ALSO BY LINDSAY HUNTER

Ugly Girls

Don't Kiss Me

Daddy's

EAT ONLY WHEN YOU'RE HUNGRY

EAT ONLY WHEN YOU'RE HUNGRY

LINDSAY HUNTER

FARRAR, STRAUS AND GIROUX   NEW YORK

Farrar, Straus and Giroux
18 West 18th Street, New York 10011

Printed in the United States of America
First edition, 2017

Heartfelt thanks are given to the band Typhoon for permission to reprint their lyrics.

Library of Congress Cataloging-in-Publication Data
Names: Hunter, Lindsay, 1980– author.
Title: Eat only when you're hungry / Lindsay Hunter.
Description: First edition. | New York : Farrar, Straus and Giroux, 2017.
Identifiers: LCCN 2016053074 | ISBN 9780374146153 (hardback) |
    ISBN 9780374715991 (e-book)
Subjects: BISAC: FICTION / Literary. | FICTION / Psychological.
Classification: LCC PS3608.U5943 E28 2017 | DDC 813/.6—dc23
LC record available at https://lccn.loc.gov/2016053074

Designed by Abby Kagan

Our books may be purchased in bulk for promotional, educational, or business
use. Please contact your local bookseller or the Macmillan Corporate and Premium
Sales Department at 1-800-221-7945, extension 5442, or by e-mail at
MacmillanSpecialMarkets@macmillan.com.

www.fsgbooks.com
www.twitter.com/fsgbooks • www.facebook.com/fsgbooks

10 9 8 7 6 5 4 3 2 1

Oh, what am I waiting for?
A spell to be cast or for it to be broken
At the very last
Some wild ghost from my past comes to split me
    wide open, oh
—Typhoon, "Common Sentiments"

EAT ONLY WHEN YOU'RE HUNGRY

It was too late to be a lunch, too early to be a dinner, this disappointing collection of food Greg was packing. He was leaving in the odd smear of time between the markers of his day. Not in the morning, not in the night. Not even in the midday. After lunch, before dinner. The sun was out but getting lazy. Everything starting to give over, accepting that this day's moment was swiftly passing. Maybe that was why he finally left. He had to get away from the giving over, for once. His son had been missing three weeks.

He was packing a meal using what he had in the fridge. A buttered heel of bread, a rhombus of stiff cheese, a puckered tangerine, its skin loose around the wedges inside it. When had he last bought tangerines? It had been months. Maybe a year. Sometimes what he thought was a long time passing ended up being only a few weeks. *Hey, when was that, last summer? Last Christmas?* And his wife answering, *Honey, that was only just last month.* So who could know when anything actually happened? When he was a child he often had to mark time for himself. *Today is Tuesday, that I know for sure. At least I know that for sure.* He was already looking forward to ignoring the lunch, stopping somewhere along the way, having a conversation with a waitress. *I'm looking for my son.* What came next? Shock? Admiration? He liked anticipating these kinds of things.

The house was implacable. Quiet and unaffected. When he left, for all the time he'd be gone, the items in the house would stay in the same place. The house was not asking him for anything; the house wasn't begging him to stay. Instead it was watching him go.

"Couch," he whispered. "Ottoman." Marking time, marking stasis. Then he said his own name: "Greg." He could just as easily have said the other names he was known by: *Honey. Gregory. Dad.* But at the end of the day, he thought of himself as only Greg. The buttery yellow light coming in through the plate-glass windows, at least, offered its confetti of dust. A stingy fanfare. His wife dusted often, almost daily, but sometimes you can't win for losing.

You can't win for losing; there he was. His son. Greg Junior. GJ. Had he said it to GJ, or had GJ said it to him? And when? On how many occasions? GJ as a child, crying over a bloody knee. GJ on the phone, calling from rehab. GJ drunk on the couch. On Couch. Likely they had said it to each other, neither truly listening. GJ with his big paw hands, his oily T-shirts, his face getting fleshy, then gaunt, then fleshy again. Beautiful boy, my beautiful boy. Greg's eyes felt warm. But was he crying for himself or for GJ? Did he think he should cry or did he actually want to cry? These were the thoughts that kept him from the trip for the past three weeks. For his whole life. That kept him from life. Again he felt like crying, but stopped himself, his throat pained, feeling stretched like it was making room for something. He didn't feel allowed to cry just yet.

He had seen a woman on one of those Saturday-night crime shows talking about her own missing child. *I know she's alive,* the woman said, tears erupting from her eyes, *I feel it inside. I know she knows I'm looking for her and I won't ever, ever stop.* Greg didn't have that same certainty. He could never feel absolutely certain about anything, least of all GJ, who felt as elusive and slippery as his own beating heart. But he felt sure, objectively, that he should never, ever stop looking for GJ, even if GJ was standing right in front of him, right this minute.

He put the lunch into one of the huge Ziploc baggies his wife saved and placed it by the door so he could grab it on the way out. The grandfather clock made a few halfhearted tones: it was 3:15. He hurried upstairs to pack a bag. The bedroom always smelled familiar, sweet and clothy. His and his wife's scent, their signature. Did they leave it behind them at restaurants, at church? Was the smell the same for her as it was for him? Sometimes he felt exhausted by all the not knowing, by all the wondering. Wandering.

The oval full-length mirror next to the bed offered him a framed portrait of himself, standing in his exhausted slippers, his calves still strong, though too pale, and disturbingly hairless. The frayed hem of the purple gym shorts he wore daily now, because their elastic was shot, and because they stopped the laborious swinging of his balls, caged them in a calming inner mesh pouch he had come to love. The XXXL undershirt, the V of his chest hair, still mostly brown, something he never failed to notice or feel thankful for. His belly straining at the shirt, pushing out out out, like it was pleased to meet the world. Greg often attempted to quantify its heft: a belly pregnant with triplets; the hull of a small boat, taking on water; a laundry sack filled with beer. He carried it around, this heavy impostor, day after day, his back giving and giving. There, too, were his hands, thicker than they had been when he was a young man, when his fingers were long and his knuckles seemed an afterthought, not the bulgy crooks they were now. His acned neck; he never had figured out how to avoid shaving rash. He had tried steam, lotions, shaving in the other direction, all to no avail. And the large anvil of his head and face, his chin and neck connected by a flap of flesh, a sheet on the line that had grown into the pin and the grass. He could see the pores in his cheeks and nose from where he was standing, his face sprouting leaks and caving into sinkholes, consuming itself. The gnarled, tortured dough of his nose. His hazel eyes, which could still appear blue or green under the right circumstances but were always too wet-looking, like he was on the perpetual verge of a sneeze. The jagged hedge of hair, graying but still thick, a small mercy. He took it all in, as he did when he could stand to, *If this is what GJ has to look forward to in his old age* . . . and then he looked away, thankful to have a task at hand.

He found a crumpled duffel bag under the bed, shoved clothes and his toothbrush inside it. More than enough socks. He'd read a war novel once that said wearing wet and dirty socks was worse than getting shot. He decided he needed to throw in a pair of nail clippers as well. Then he decided to bring his father's pocketknife, though it was dull and mostly for show at this point. An item of remembrance. Another marker of time.

"Honey?" His wife was in the doorway; he hadn't heard her come in. Crisp white button-down tucked into a flowered skirt;

feet planted shoulder-width in their white sneakers, sturdy freckled calves. Hair pinned back out of her eyes. Purse snug under her arm. Nothing worrisome; nothing out of place. His wife was a relief to his brain. Everything about her made sense.

"When was the last time we bought tangerines?" he asked. He had a ball of socks in each hand, and it felt good to have something to hold, to have a purpose for each hand.

His wife took a step into the room, then stopped. "Well, I was just at the store, should I have . . ." She looked at the socks in his hands, at the duffel on the bed.

"I was just wondering how long it's been." He transferred one sock ball to the other hand, so he could have a free hand for gesturing. Natural gesturing.

"I guess I don't really remember," she said, putting her purse onto the chair by the door, where it relaxed and slumped in on itself, like a teenager. Not remembering was often good enough for his wife, and though he admired this about her it also made him feel panicked on occasion. "I believe we had some in a salad about a month or so ago. Remember the night we had salmon steaks?" She took another step toward him. His wife knew he felt more comfortable knowing; he could see her trying to bring up the memory, force it into existence.

He did remember, though he remembered raspberries in the salad that night. He slotted in the tangerine wedges instead and decided to leave it be. He had only brought it up to buy himself some time.

"You're going after GJ," she said, sitting on the arm of the chair. "I thought we talked about this."

"We did, we did."

"You know that he might not want to be found, Greg, right? And if you do find him he might . . . you might not want to see him that way." She had picked up her purse again, was moving the straps in her hands like she was trying to figure out what they were made of. She was not GJ's mother, though she had mothered him when GJ stayed with them, and Greg sometimes had ugly thoughts about how she could never understand. She had once had to stick her fingers down GJ's throat, had caught his vomit in her shirt the way one catches falling apples. She had said soothing things, patted his back, led him into the shower, but then she had not slept in bed with Greg that night, or the night after that. They did this to each other: traded rage back and forth when GJ wasn't able to take it.

"He knows I'll come for him, Deb. I can't ever, ever stop coming for him." He felt ridiculous saying it out loud. Overly dramatic. But Deb was crying now, holding the backs of her wrists up to her cheeks, so maybe it had been the right thing to say.

"I just want to know when it will end," she said, her voice pinched, almost whining. She was not a whiner. They had both retired early, within six months of each other, had made promises about cooking classes and tennis and trips. *We could take naps,* Deb said, and then in the same exact tone had said, *We can have sex in the middle of the day, under the dining table.* They had rejoiced in leaving the pressures of work behind. They were both accountants, she for a firm and he for a small group of wealthy idiots. One of his clients, a young man who owned three barbecue restaurants, had once asked him if laundering money literally meant washing it. But there was pressure in idleness, too. Mostly they kept the TV on and went from room to room, like they were playing a slow game of tag. Deb had invented reasons to leave the house: daily grocery shopping, book club, swim lessons. But for Greg life had started to reveal itself as a series of distractions. It felt real only when he was quiet and still, emptied. Life felt real only when he felt like a ghost. *Ha!* Another dramatic thing. Well, now GJ needed him, and that was a welcome distraction from himself.

When your son is an addict you can think things like *He is missing and that is a welcome distraction* and not feel like a monster. Can't you? He had become inured, maybe. Was that even the right word?

"It will end," Greg said. "This is the end." It was certainly an end to *something*, even if it was only the end to the day.

Deb sniffed three quick times, getting herself together in her efficient way. GJ's mother was the kind to let her face get messy, to fall into itself, to let the snot flow right into her open mouth as she cried. To use her face, her *feelings*, as weapons against him. He felt a surge of love for Deb; they were the same kind of person. He understood her and she understood him. He almost asked her to come along; in fact, it had been what he meant to say even as he began speaking. But instead he said: "I won't be gone long." Which was possibly a lie. And Deb would never come along, anyway. There was the matter of the errands she needed to run, the dusting, the swimming, the dishes, the endless circuit of *keeping up*. Greg could not keep up. He no longer wanted to. In this they were diverging, like someone had switched the tracks at the last minute, separating their train cars. They were waving at each other from windows, promising to meet up soon. So they were both lying.

"I don't even know where you think he is." Deb's voice had righted itself, unclenched. She was ready to move on from the emotions to the details. "Will you take the Volvo?"

"No, no," he said. They only had the one car. "You keep the Volvo. I'm going to rent an RV."

Deb stood up, smoothed her skirt, which accordioned back

into wrinkles immediately. "Well, I'll drive you to town, at least," she said. Like the house, she wasn't begging him to stay. She was watching him go. He wished he could see himself from her eyes; wished he could be in her brain, which was probably already on to planning the next few weeks, all the things she'd do while he was gone. Plant things. Dig things up. Arrange and rearrange. Grocery shopping. Satisfaction. No staring just to the left of the raging television, no letting noise just wash over her. They had never had sex under the dining table, and he thought maybe he should attempt it now, before he left. But that felt like a planting all on its own. He'd be exhausted after; he had a sudden vision of all the shifting and wiping they'd have to do once it was finished. And during, there'd be all the thoughts they were having, apart from each other, about each other. Then he'd tell himself he'd leave the next day and then he never would.

"Deb," he said. She was looking around, her eyes searching out something to add to his duffel, something necessary, logical, something he could be grateful to her for. Above everything, Deb valued being useful. What did he value above everything? *Oblivion*.

Deb looked at him, waiting. He cleared his throat. "I took the last of the cheese."

"Oh," she said. "I can get some more after I drop you off . . . Where should I drop you off?"

He didn't know, but these were the things Deb was good for. She logged on to the Internet and found a company a half-hour's drive away called Go West. By the time he was coming downstairs with his duffel bag she'd rented him a vehicle.

"They call it a nineteen-footer. It's a compact," she said, a pad of paper balanced on her knees, her ankles together neatly. She tapped her notes lightly with her pen. "Since it's just you I figured that was okay. Plus you're not good at parking larger vehicles." She was referring to the time, years ago, when they were moving GJ into a new apartment nearby and Greg had backed the U-Haul into a motorcycle. In fact, it had terrified him; even now he found himself snapping awake after a dream where he'd backed the U-Haul into Deb or GJ or a small child that was probably also GJ.

"Thank you," he said. She was still sitting, looking up at him with her eyes wide the way she tended to when she was being a know-it-all, something he found endearing. She looked almost childlike. Deb, in her mid-fifties, with threads of silver shooting through her blond hair. He could see what she looked like as a child. Pretty and serious.

"You know," she was saying. She handed Greg her paper and pen; she often handed things to him to put away, maybe because it spoke of their partnership, their two sides to the same shell. "I think this might be a good thing." The windows behind her showed the tall trees they had in the yard, oaks and elms and a few firs, decades old, older than GJ, swaying like her backup dancers. "I think . . ." She was starting to cry again, Greg saw, tears surfacing and sliding down, one after another. He put his hand on her shoulder, but then she laughed, a half bark that brought her hand up to hold the other half in. "Greg, I think I might feel relieved." She laughed harder now, her mouth open, looking into his face the way people do when they want to make sure their partners are getting the joke. Greg took his hand away, but it hung in the air like it was the one part of his body that wasn't made out of flesh. Like it was a metal claw or a balloon. He couldn't figure out what to do with his hand, or how he should help Deb, or if she even needed help. Her shoulders shook; she was making a silent cackling noise.

"Relief is good, right?" Greg said. He also felt relieved, was the thing. But he and Deb had an unspoken agreement not to call a spade a spade when it came to moments like these. People had complicated emotions: that was understood between them when they began getting serious twenty years ago, and there was no need to discuss it. He had gotten fat in retirement. He had gotten slow. Even more tired than he ever had been working. He carried his lethargic body as far as it could go; even lying down felt like he was being asked to wear a suit made of mud. He felt assaulted by the possibilities of the day, exposed by the sun. Deb had quickly learned to call him half an hour before coming home in the afternoon so he'd have time to rush around and tidy up, change out of his pajamas, brush his teeth, pretend he hadn't been sitting in the same place for hours and hours. There was no need to discuss it; Deb understood and Greg understood that she understood and he was grateful not to have to explain himself, because he didn't even know where to begin. Because how can you start at oblivion?

Deb voicing her relief was a change. Almost a betrayal. But he didn't have time to get into it; suddenly he had to get out.

"It's okay to feel relieved," he said.

"I just mean . . . you're doing something. I'm relieved to see you doing something. You packed a lunch!" She was holding her hand out, palm up, to where he'd dumped his Ziploc of fridge orphans.

"I did. I even buttered a piece of bread." This made her laugh even harder, her elbows on her knees, both hands over her mouth. He laughed, too, both of them laughing at Greg, this Greg goof who was basically a lump with eyes.

Deb inhaled, a big shuddering gulp. She'd had her fill of

laughing for now. She took his hand, the metal claw, enfolded it into the soft warmth of her palms. "But Greg, I just want you to know that GJ is beyond us now. This will probably not end well, do you understand?" Her voice was so tender, so gentle. She was trying to ready him for destruction. GJ had never gone missing for more than a couple of days, and even then it had been easy to find him in three phone calls, tops. She was telling him that GJ was dead, or as good as.

"I understand."

He did not agree. He did not understand. One summer evening many lifetimes ago, he'd been the one to tuck GJ into bed. The boy excited, a treat to have Greg all to himself. The boy reaching under his pillow, whispering, *Dad, look what God has been leaving for me in the yard.* A baggie of spider's eggs, brown and fuzzy. Greg had yanked the bag from the boy's hands, run through the house, stomped the baggie to a pulp on the driveway before he'd thought to explain to the boy what he'd actually collected. GJ crying so hard that he made no sound. Openmouthed grief. Greg had had a fight with GJ's mother that night. His emotions were right there. His rage. He'd been so young then. Why hadn't he just emptied the eggs into the yard? How could GJ be suddenly dead? None of it computed, none of it fell into place.

Deb was standing now. "When you're ready," she said. GJ had gone through a phase of mimicking her mannered ways. Napkin in lap. Elbows poised, just off the table. Saying *Many thanks* instead of *Thank you.* Then he had entered a phase of despising her every move, as if her way of living, her clean, ordered, thoughtful way of living, was in direct insult to his. There were moments when Greg felt the same way. *When you're ready.* Like he was one of her clients during tax season. But then she reached out, ran a fingertip across his cheek, cold and soft as a paintbrush. He hadn't known he was crying, despite himself, until then. He felt foolish, judged by the air he was breathing. Simpering old man. Ottoman rigid with embarrassment for him. "I'm ready," he said.

The RV seemed made for men like him, men whose asses needed room to spread, men whose backs zinged at the sight of a golf club. The driver's seat was as wide as two seats in the Volvo, skinned in a plush gray something or other, and felt four feet deep with cushion. The headrest stayed out of his way but was at the ready whenever Greg needed cradling. He imagined having this seat removed and installed in his living room, bolted to the floor, in front of but not too close to the TV.

The vehicle smelled like someone had smoked a pack of cigarettes while spritzing a whole canister of air freshener, a comforting smell actually, something very akin to the bathroom at Mick's Bar & Grille, where he used to take clients and Deb and GJ. On occasion he'd go by himself, sitting at the bar yelling orders for beers and fries over John Cougar Mellencamp and Bob Seger and pretending not to notice himself in the mirror behind the whiskey, though he found it hard to tear his eyes away. He looked like pictures of himself as a boy, as a young man, as a middle-aged man in the family pictures Deb insisted on, but he still couldn't get a handle on *what he looked like*. Even now, in the RV's rearview, he could see slices of his face—forehead, nose and cheeks, mouth and chin—but never everything at once. He had read a *Reader's Digest* article about face blindness in a doctor's waiting room, but had been called in before he could finish it. He never found out if people could have face blindness for themselves. He supposed he could google it. It's what Deb would do. Sometimes it was nice to have easily solved problems remain unsolved, for those days when it all felt like a mystery. He had more and more of those lately, but Google didn't have an answer for everything.

He and Deb had hugged goodbye outside the open door of the RV, a long, full-contact hug that Deb had ended using her normal signal: a flutter of pats between his shoulder blades. He'd attempted to pat her as well, but his hand was in a fist over the RV keys, and he ended up pounding her a little.

"You call me," Deb said, pointing at his pocket, where he kept his phone, a black square that flipped open. "Keep it charged."

She had waved as she was getting into the Volvo, then called out, "I'll be fine!" She hadn't turned to wave as she drove away. She would be fine. She always was. He imagined that's what she'd say when he was on his deathbed. He didn't know where these unkind thoughts came from; she didn't deserve them, but *I'll be fine* was a strange thing to say at that moment, there was no doubt about that. The last time they'd discussed GJ's disappearance, Greg wanting to go over every possibility (except for death), it had ground to a silent halt, both of them spent, sitting on opposite ends of the couch. Suddenly Deb spoke: "A man in my swim class, Reggie, I think his name is, said I have nice legs for a woman of my maturity. My *maturity.* Isn't that funny?" She wanted him to think it was a story about how the man had pronounced the word: *ma-tour-a-tee.* But Greg knew better. It was not a warning, it was a fact. Deb could find what she needed anywhere. She was nothing if not resourceful. Instead of scaring him, it made him feel calm, more at peace.

He had eased the RV out of its parking space, maneuvered it around the tricky curve in the lot and out onto the main road, all in time to see the Volvo pulling a U-turn at the light and going back toward home. Ships in the night. Vehicles in the evening. The RV was too high up for him to be able to see her face, to notice anything other than her arm, the neat white cuff of her shirt unfurling, blooming like a hidden Kleenex. When he reached the light it was red. The RV needed a few pumps of the brake to fully stop. At each corner, facing each other like warriors painted in lurid yellows and reds, there was a Popeye's, an Arby's, a Bob Evans, an AutoZone. He remembered that he'd forgotten his lunch. He remembered that he'd forgotten. Ha! That should be on his tombstone.

Up ahead was the turnoff for the highway that would take him slightly west and then south. A few miles past that was the highway that would take him north. He took the first one, because it connected to the second one a hundred miles down, long enough for him to know for sure if he wanted to change his mind. If he didn't, he'd reach GJ's mother's condo after about ten hours. He hadn't called ahead. They had called each other, texted, both asking if the other had heard from GJ. But she didn't seem as concerned as she might have been. She didn't know where he was, wasn't interested in joining Greg in the speculation. It felt like something was off, like she wasn't telling him the whole story. Or maybe that's what he hoped was true. So he didn't plan on calling ahead. Some people were better caught off guard.

Greg had been born in Virginia, grown up in Denver, met GJ's mother at college in Arizona, settled their uneasy family in Florida, and then fled with Deb, following job opportunities to Greensboro and then Birmingham, before finally retiring, almost on a whim, to the mountains of West Virginia. GJ's mother had stayed in Florida, which was as hot as Arizona but somehow worse, and Greg had come to think of their time together as a journey between two poles in hell: one dry and one humid.

GJ's mother. Marie. A common name, and now any time he met a Marie he assumed the placid, friendly face on the woman was a mask for the dangerous rapids of emotion underneath. He first saw her at a party, laughing among a group of guys, holding a cup of punch like everyone else but never, ever drinking from it. It was why he noticed her in the first place: she'd gone to fill up her cup but had ladled the punch back into the bowl, a clever trick that kept her sober as a church all night long. Greg got so drunk that night that he fell asleep outside his own dorm room, drooling onto the stiff carpet and waking only when his roommate opened the door, found him, and tried dragging him inside. He saw Marie at the library weeks later, and it brought the night back to him, how she'd seemed to be enjoying herself without drinking, how for him blacking out had been the point. Only the night before seeing her at the library, Greg had allowed a nerdy guy in a raincoat to place a tiny paper stamp under his tongue, had let it dissolve while watching the guy's enormous Adam's apple moving up and down his thin neck like he was trying to dislodge it. "There we go," the guy said, and Greg thought he meant he had succeeded in swallowing it down, his neck finally smooth and knobless, finally.

She was leaned back in a chair, reading the newspaper the way his father always had, opened in front of her face like a display of normalcy in a forgotten museum.

"Hey," he said. And when she didn't immediately respond, he said, "Anything good?"

She bent a corner, looked up at him. Her eyes were black, like they were all pupil, all-seeing. Something he hadn't noticed the night of the party. She was wearing glasses, big as windowpanes. "Do you mean me?" she asked.

For a moment he wondered if he *did* mean her. Was he remembering this woman correctly? "I think I saw you," he said, which was the absolute truth. "At a party at Dov's apartment a few weeks ago?"

She folded the paper down, putting it to rest on her lap, smoothing it like a piece of laundry. "Are you the guy I borrowed cab fare from?" she asked. "You don't look like him. That guy was blond."

Later Greg would remember how they were both trying to place each other, how they both couldn't quite be sure who they were recognizing, and bitterly think to himself, *I should have known.*

"That wasn't me, no. I was the guy who . . ." But he didn't know who he'd been that night. *I was the guy who was partying. I was the guy who got so drunk he became faceless. I was any guy on any night.* "I was the guy who mixed the punch." This was true; he had mixed it one or two times. To mix was to add more alcohol.

"I'll take your word for it," she said. "Do you want to sit down? Or are you waiting for the paper?" She held it out to him.

He wanted to tell her he'd been fascinated by her, laughing like one of the guys, fooling everyone with her punch trick. He wanted to ask her why she did it. Why come to a party and not drink? He couldn't imagine anything worse than hanging out with a bunch of drunk people if you yourself weren't drunk. It had been what college was to him: a place to let go, let go completely. To reach a place beyond inhibition, beyond thought. His mother's voice: *Don't embarrass us.* A throwaway thing she said often. Now he was somewhere she couldn't even see him. It felt like a hidden fortune he couldn't spend fast enough.

"I already read it," he said. "But I'd like to take you to dinner, or coffee, or to a movie sometime?"

"How about all three?" she said, smiling, laughing at him even. "How do you know I don't have a boyfriend?"

He looked around him, suddenly worried she did have a boyfriend who was watching all of this happen, watching him make a fool of himself in front of a strange girl whom he couldn't stop staring at. His jaw felt tired; he'd been clenching it all night long, working through the high, and his mouth felt sour, unclean. He'd showered and brushed his teeth, come to the library to study, but in front of her now he felt like a homeless man hoping to pass as a lawyer.

"I don't have a boyfriend," she finally said. "And coffee makes me crazy. But we could go for lunch now, if you want."

He did the math quickly in his head. He had a few quarters in his pocket, a couple dollars shoved into his economics textbook at home, hidden from his roommate. In the three seconds before he'd asked her out he'd figured he'd have time to go home and get his money, to make more in fact—he was days away from being paid for the job he had cleaning classrooms in the math buildings on campus.

"I have a sandwich in my bag," Marie said. "We could each eat a half. Plus an apple." She seemed to read his mind. Over time Greg would learn that Marie was a master at watching people think, intuiting their every whim. It was a talent that during their years together held him fascinated, afraid, and, finally, disgusted.

He didn't know if he should sit, wait for her to pass him his half, or suggest going outside, finding a shady tree, somewhere soft to sit. Marie put the paper on the chair next to her, stood, and hefted her schoolbag over her shoulder. That answered that. All his life, Greg appreciated people who just made the decision for him. He and Marie ended up on the library steps, because it was Arizona and even a shady tree couldn't shield them from the sun pushing its heat down on them, that ceiling of oven. And at least the library's porch had fans, lazily wheeling above them, offering a slice of air about every three minutes. Greg could feel his body slowly becoming a liquid, melting in front of this girl, his sweat probably smelling of beer.

"My dad didn't want me to come here," she was saying.

"Come to Arizona?" Greg asked. The sandwich was egg salad with little bits of pickle and olive. It had been sitting in her bag long enough to become enfolded in its own scent, warm and a bit too moist.

She laughed, revealing a fleck of black pepper clinging to her incisor. "No, I mean come to college." She ran her tongue over her teeth. He wondered if he'd been staring at the fleck, if that's how she knew, or if it was one of those things people did just to be sure. Just to be sure, he ran his tongue over his teeth, too. "He thought I should stay home and help around the house."

"Ah," Greg said, which was what he said when he wanted to acknowledge what was said without going too far. He wanted to say that sounded like an old-fashioned, selfish thing for a father to say to a child, but his roommate had once said something similar about Greg's parents and Greg had wanted to set his cot on fire with the lighter they hid in the pencil cup.

"Sometimes I feel bad about it," she said. She laughed again; the pepper fleck was still there, holding strong. He waited for her to run her tongue along her teeth again, but she didn't. She took her glasses off instead, reached over and tugged his T-shirt sleeve a bit until she had enough cloth, and used it to clean her glasses. Greg had grown up in a house where you hugged only on birthdays or solemn occasions, where when friends came over they had to ask for a glass of water or juice. He had friends whose mothers expected you to saunter into the kitchen and make yourself a snack, who hugged him and didn't tell him to take off his shoes or ask him when he was going to grow up. He had always felt alarmed by this kind of closeness, on guard. The kind of relaxation, the comfort in his own body that they expected of him was bizarre. Eventually he decided to go to the fridge every single time, even if he wasn't thirsty or hungry, simply to trick them into believing he could be that kind of person. *Hello, I am simply a human like you are a human. I did not count the steps it takes to get from the back door to the kitchen, and I definitely feel one hundred and ten percent normal taking your last Fanta.* Marie clearly grew up in that kind of house, or at least a house where you took people's comfort for granted. Where you could meet someone and then twenty minutes later be using his T-shirt to clean your fingerprints and cheek smudges and dust off of your glasses. It felt beyond intimate to Greg. He would have been less shocked if she had reached over and cradled his penis in her hand. But there was the other feeling, too, the feeling he got when his friends' mothers said things like *Now, Greg, you're staying for supper, right?* or *I remembered that you like these kinds of potato chips the best* or *How did that test go?* Most of him was on guard, calculating his responses. But a small part of him was touched, genuinely touched, his throat closing a little and his face wanting to crumple. What was that? They accepted him. He was one of them. He wouldn't be alone forever. His mother, ashing into a tea saucer. *Nobody loves you like your mother.* Something like that.

Marie had accepted him. She could clean her glasses on his sleeve and tell him about the selfish things her father said to her. He was a shield, a fort of blankets in which she could confide her every thought. "Don't feel bad," he said. He was thinking of his mother, of her twiglike wrists and small face. There were seventeen steps from the sidewalk up to the library. From the top of the steps to the front door was between ten and twelve steps, depending. *Don't feel bad.* It's what he told himself often.

"I do and I don't," Marie said. "Like this one time, I was helping my dad sort his papers. He sells magazine subscriptions, sometimes. I was sorting the subscribed from the unsubscribed. And I was thinking, 'Well, I could do this. This isn't all that painful. And maybe one day I could get promoted to partner in his little business, or something. And I could still be me.' Isn't that strange?

'I could still be me.' So clearly, if you have to convince yourself that you could still be you by doing something you had previously dreaded or rejected, then maybe that is actually not the best life choice." Marie said things like *life choice. Realized. Fully realized.* She spoke in self-help speak but did not read those kinds of books or travel in those kinds of circles. She just was that kind of person, the kind to consider herself, to self-scrutinize. To look at life like it was a one-million-piece puzzle. Like there was a chance at solving it.

"So I feel bad because I couldn't accept what I was saying to myself, but I don't feel bad because I think my father would like me even less if I didn't defy him. I really think that sometimes." She threw the remaining third of her sandwich-half like a Frisbee. We watched a squirrel approach it, edging up like a guy at a party trying to see if there was anything there. The sun was beginning to set, drawing up its stinging cloak, though in some ways the night's heat was even worse, because it all felt closer. Inescapable.

"I don't think my mother ever liked me," Greg said, surprising himself. He didn't want the afternoon to end, maybe. Or he felt dared to trade a truth for a truth.

"Doesn't everyone feel that way?"

"Oh. Do they?" Greg thought of his friends' mothers again. His friends never seemed to feel that strongly about them one way or the other. They simply *were.* They appeared when they were needed and they disappeared back into their own days when they weren't. One asked him to call her Mona. Another said he could call her Mrs. Helen. "Do you think your mother never liked you?"

"My mother is a very depressed person," she said, as if this answered the question. "I bet your mother is a very depressed person, too. I think our mothers' generation is a very depressed generation."

She said it as if it were a known fact, something throwaway, as bland as *Christopher Columbus discovered America.*

His mother never slept in. In fact, he sometimes wondered if she slept at all. She always had her makeup on, was always dressed neatly in bright colors. She smoked all day and drank starting at 5:00 on the dot. She had her friend come over to set her hair twice a week. She didn't look like what he imagined a depressed person looked like: greasy, half-asleep, hateful. His mother laughed often. She threw dinner parties and went to the club for drinks. She kissed Greg's father full on the lips every morning and every night when he came home. It was more that she treated Greg like a guest who had long overstayed his welcome. But maybe he was overreacting. Maybe every child wondered if he or she was the sole source of regret in their parents' lives. He had once asked his mother what was for dinner. *Go out and pick yourself up a mommy and ask her.* To be fair, she was two gins in when he'd asked.

"You're probably right," Greg said. Now he wanted the afternoon wrapped up. Marie could do that: pull him in, mesmerize him, and then say or do something that left him blinking, wondering where he was and how he'd gotten there. He had never told anyone how he felt about his mother, maybe because a small part of him worried he was being overdramatic, and here Marie was confirming just that. Pull, push, pull push, a decade-and-a-half carnival ride that started under an angry sun one afternoon during college.

"I'm not saying it's easy," she said. She put her hand on his knee. Her hand was cold and dry, which made her seem even more unreal, and he worried his knee would begin to sweat and tarnish her perfect doll's hand. "It's not easy being someone's child, is it? Everyone always talks about how hard being a parent is. Being a child is worse, because you have to survive despite your parents. And you have to make them proud but also forge your own path."

Greg nodded. Her hand began to feel heavy, alien, it was all Greg could think about. He wanted to laugh, wanted to point out to Marie how everything she'd just said could have been in one of those films about how hard it was to be a teenager. In truth he'd felt like an adult trapped in a child's body his whole life. "Do you want to walk me to my dorm?" she asked. "Fair warning, I have a single, so we can be alone, but I'm a virgin."

She stood, held out a hand to help him up, but Greg felt frozen, shot through with adrenaline. Was she saying they were about to have sex? Or was she saying she was definitely not going to have sex with him? He felt his blood racing through his body while his arms and legs felt tranquilized. He felt like he was on a bad high. He wanted the coldest can of beer available. He was also a virgin.

Later Greg would think how he had seen her at a party and spoken to her for a total of thirty minutes at the library. That was it. That was all he needed to know. But sometimes knowing everything about a person can get in the way. Without Marie, no GJ. *I never asked to be born.* GJ had pulled that out of his bag of tricks on more than one occasion, usually when arguing, but sometimes when he seemed tired, beyond help. *Yes you did*, Greg wanted to say. *You were desperate to be born. You were there on the steps that day, like a gas. Drugging us. It's not my fault you can't handle it. Who can?*

They went back to Marie's dorm room, walking down the seventeen steps and across the choked and crackling lawn. She lived in the smart-kids dorm, all brick and scrollwork and columns, the student at the front desk nodding and then looking away without asking just what was going on here. Marie had a framed chalkboard on her door, an empty piece of string where a nub of chalk had once been. A smear of white dust. What did it say before it was erased? "I'm not going to have sex with you," she said. "Not today, anyway." But she was wrong. The silence in her room, her broken desk chair, the bed a magnet for sitting and then lying, they didn't stand a chance. Both of them probably thinking, *Well, let's just get it over with.* She pulled his shirt up; she put her cold hand on his hip. He placed his lips on hers. Mrs. Helen standing in her kitchen, hands spread on the bar that faced into the den, hunched over and staring at her son and his friends like a coach at half-time. *And don't* ever *put your tongue in a girl's mouth uninvited. You hear me?* It had been unclear what motivated this moment of advice, possibly a commercial that had been popular around then, where a woman uses a new toothpaste and men can't stop walking up to her and kissing her, tasting her. Greg had never seen her so serious, and it stuck with him. So he put his lips to Marie's lips and waited for his invitation, which came via the tip of her tongue, darting out like the probe of some deep-sea creature. *Anyone out there?* He wondered how a girl this beautiful and strange could be so inexperienced, so untouched. He put his hand on her shoulder, then her elbow, and then her waist, wanting to give her his whole tongue, both of them tasting like egg salad and salt. She lay back and he moved over her, positioning them into a pair of parallel planes, the position of the inexperienced. Looked into her black eyes, the sweat at her hairline while she pushed her jeans down and then his. It was not an easy thing, pushing in, past the exasperated barrier, moving among blood, especially with a gasping stranger. And even then, trying to drown out the numbers in his head, trying not to count the thrusts, trying not to lose himself in the rule of threes. If something adds up to three, six, or nine, then it is divisible by three. He lost count after fifteen. By then he felt swallowed by her, wrapped in her hair and arms and that deep dark entryway he plunged into again and again, like a boy who has just learned the joy of the high jump. It wasn't just that it felt good; it was that it *felt*. He was all sensation, like his body was a giant tongue. He looked down at her to see if she felt the same way, but her eyes were closed. Sounds escaped his lips, grunts and yips like he'd never made before. Marie mostly sighed, but not necessarily in a bad way. He told himself, reviewing it all later, they'd both entered the void, if only for a moment. *Void* has four letters. Not divisible by three. But *avoids* has six letters. Divisible by three down to two. After that afternoon in her dorm, they were two, and then a few years later they became three, and then they became one and one and one.

The sack of burgers Greg had purchased from the Krystal was half full now, and probably cold, but he knew they'd taste heavenly in the night when he wasn't sure if he could push on. They'd be like energy tablets, little sliders of grease and grace, something to look forward to. He and GJ used to get a sack each, it was their little secret from Deb, and the burgers had to be eaten outside the car or else she'd smell it. They'd sit on the trunk or the hood or at a picnic bench if they felt like driving to the park to watch the muddy water lapping at the shore and the ducks swiveling their necks, impatient for a morsel. Laughing at their rudeness, their open demands. Having a secret with his son like that felt like he was doing something right. A necessary indulgence, this harmless nothing in the scheme of things, that sideways grin GJ would allow when Greg slowed the car to turn in to the Krystal's parking lot. *Shh*, they'd whisper to each other. *Don't tell Deb.*

Sometimes he did tell Deb. It felt good to recap, to revisit the bonding, the afternoon's new heap of cement, make sure it was dry. And, sure, to give himself a little credit for doing something right. When he thought of GJ's childhood he remembered yelling a lot. And when he wasn't yelling, he didn't have a lot to say to the boy. What they don't tell you is it's all work. Parenting, marriage. They're both jobs. Nothing ever seemed easy. But those moments eating that shitty food and grinning at each other, that felt easy.

Sometimes Greg had to remind himself that GJ was almost thirty years old now. When he himself was thirty he was married with a child and a mortgage on that tiny place they'd bought when they first moved to Florida. The Shed is what they called it. It looked like a game piece, an approximation of what a house might look like. Square and squat, the front of the house flat, shutters fixed to the sides of the two windows. The door flush with the rest of the house, no porch, no shelter from the sun or the mean rains Florida liked to bestow out of nowhere.

Still, when he thought of GJ he thought of a boy, or a young man. Not the father-aged adult mess that he seemed to be now. GJ's hairline receding, his teeth shifting, crowding each other, stubble staining his face. He was aging, like Greg had aged. Of all the disappointments a father can have in his son, that had to be up there. Bodies aged and gave out. No one could stop it. Even if he'd tried as hard as he could, even if he had really done his best as a father, Greg could never stop it.

A school bus passed him, the children with their hands plastered on the windows like starfish, a dark-haired boy licking the window, another child waving at Greg and smiling big, like they knew each other. He waved and the child threw her head back and laughed, pointing at him, like what a dummy, this guy out here waving back at me, this guy practicing a *societal norm*, as Marie would say. He was about five hundred miles from her, enough time to assemble the armor he'd need, inside and out. He and Deb had a brick fireplace at the house, and he imagined bricking himself up like that: brick inside and brick outside and a fire going straight up the middle and out the top. Not whooshing out and catching anything. Nothing dangerous or untoward. It had been years since he'd seen Marie, probably since the first time they took GJ to rehab. They'd done it together, then, as a family. He and Deb in the Volvo, Marie behind them in her Kia. GJ switching cars when they stopped for gas or to pee, drinking a flat bottle of rum with a straw, then moving to a Big Gulp invaded by vodka. It felt like a monumental journey. It felt like they were driving GJ to health. All they had to do was drop him off, act like a support system, show that they were there for him as a unit, and thirty days later he'd be okay. *You know,* Marie had said, *I read that the chances of relapse after rehab are so large that it's almost guaranteed.* They were standing by their cars, none of them certain if they should wait some more, if they were supposed to go in and put sheets on GJ's bed, put his toothbrush in the holder, put his T-shirts and underwear in drawers for him, eat dinner with him, find a more official way of saying goodbye than the one they'd actually had: watching him be led by the elbow through double doors that made an angry buzz as they closed behind him. GJ had put two fingers up in a wave, but he hadn't turned around, hadn't given them his face, and Greg wondered if they were doing the right thing or if GJ was being pushed further into the hole he hid from them in, and the doors were basically agreeing with him, growling *WRONG. Wroooonnnnggg.* And in the circular drive, Marie leaning against the Volvo like it was hers, her sunglasses slightly crooked, her arms crossed, casually mentioning that this whole thing, this rehab, which had felt like salvation on the drive up, was doomed from the start. *I just think you need to be prepared.* Saying *you*. Not *we*. For Greg, it had been enough. Addicts talk about reaching bottom, and how they know the next step is death or get better, and for Greg his bottom had been watching his ex-wife, GJ's mother, once again telling him what he needed to do, not for a second dropping all pretenses and just admitting that she was sad, and sorry, and that she didn't know what to do or where to go. They took GJ to his next three rehabs separately after that. One would take him; the other would pick him up. It had been enough for both of them.

She was right, though. GJ relapsed a month after getting home. Drinking beers at dinner, offering to get one for Greg and Deb, Greg deciding beers weren't anything to worry about, as long as GJ's eyes stayed clear. And then GJ gone two whole days and Deb missing forty dollars from her wallet.

Sometimes on those afternoons with the sacks of burgers he'd let GJ have a beer. Just one. And the boy rarely finished it. *Tastes like urine*, he said once. *How do you know?* Greg asked. GJ laughing, his cheeks red. So in a way Greg had forced it on him. The pleasure of the buzz.

Greg stepped on the gas, moving the RV up from 50 to 60. Memory Lane always made him impatient. If he could just get to GJ, if he could just find him. At the very least, he'd be able to put his arms around his son. Rock bottom, but together. Together at rock bottom.

The radio was playing a song he'd heard three times in the six hours he'd been driving. *Don't you forget about me.* Greg wanted to smash the console with his fist even as he sang along. *La la la la . . .* He had to stop. He was thirsty and it was late. The streetlights along the highway whipping by him, flashes and trails, making the world feel more dark. He wasn't going to make it to Marie's all in one drive like he wanted to. He'd rest up, shower, get back on the road, arrive his best self rather than the ragged one he was dragging behind him. If GJ was at Marie's house, then he was probably safe. If he wasn't, then there was nothing a few hours of rest could change.

These were the things he said to himself, that voice inside him getting louder, more insistent, repeating these pick-up sticks of logic that made pulling over into the diner/strip club not just a decision he was making, but a necessary one. There was food there, and a Days

Inn a hundred yards off where he felt sure he could park the RV and sleep, and there were people and music and all the rest of it. He pulled into the extravagant parking lot, where they had spaces for compacts and trucks and RVs and even semis. He wasn't the only one who yearned. He was simply one among many. The ratio of cars driving by to cars parked in the lot said he was normal, just a normal man with a thirst.

He had never been good about stepping outside of his routine. When he wasn't doing what he always did it seemed like all bets were off, anything was possible; he was exposed.

He switched off the engine, the car's sudden silence hissing and loud. His shoulders ached; he'd been holding them up close to his ears. Only now could he see that driving the RV was not an easy thing, that this trip was rooting around in his body and shellacking his joints, freezing his limbs and torso and making him feel like he needed a chisel to shift in his seat.

He dialed the house. If he was going into a strip club the least he could do was call Deb first. It was just past ten o'clock. Usually by that time he'd been asleep for an hour or more, and Deb was putting down her cross-stitch or her book or switching off the TV on the odd day she actually watched something, about ready to head up and lie next to him in bed.

"Well, how's it going so far?" Caller ID meant Deb rarely answered with *Hello?*

"Fine, I stopped at the Krystal." This seemed the safer confession to make.

"Oh, Greg." At his last checkup the doctor had asked him how long he wanted to live. *How long do you want to live?* As easy as if he'd asked him, *What will you eat for dinner tonight?* He hadn't waited for Greg to answer; he'd calmly explained that Greg was killing himself faster than old age ever would, and that he needed to start walking, eating better, drinking less. The doctor's voice smooth, unbroken, like the doctor didn't even need air to speak, just rattling off this death sentence and offering Greg a way out, but only for a short while. He'd driven straight to the grocery store afterward, done the equivalent of sweeping his hand across a desk, pulling all sorts of alien fruits and vegetables into his basket. He'd even grabbed a box of green tea. Took it all home and put it away, yanking out boxes of Twinkies and packages of bacon and bricks of American cheese and the mocha-nut creamer he put in his coffee and sometimes drank straight from the bottle if Deb wasn't home.

"I know," Greg said. "I just felt like treating myself."

Deb had made a salad for dinner the night he brought home that grocery-store harvest, a bright and colorful meal that looked like a picture and made Greg's heart sink to look at it. The grape tomatoes burst in his mouth, his tongue dodging the slime; the shredded carrots tasted like earth; the radishes released a fume that snaked from his throat up to his nose and made him want to hack the mouthful onto his plate. So that's what radishes tasted like. Now he knew. They rotted at the bottom of the crisper drawer, they and the lettuce heads and the carrots in their peels. Deb pulled them out a month later, floating in their bags in what looked like lake water, scrubbed the crisper in the sink so it was clean and empty and ready for more bacon.

He guessed that's what sobriety felt like to GJ: a lurid, hopeful salad that he could not even pretend to choke down.

"Did you keep your phone charged?" Deb asked. She had decided to forgo the lecture. Lately, she'd lectured him less and less. Giving up. A relief and a warning, for Greg.

"I did," he said. "I'm going to stop for the night. I'm exhausted."

"I think that's a good idea."

They were quiet for a minute or so, listening to each other breathe. It never felt awkward to be quiet in Deb's presence. It never felt like she was waiting for him to do or say anything.

"Well, tomorrow when you eat breakfast, see if you can't find one of those smoothie places. Or get the oatmeal at Starbucks. Something to balance you out," she said. Always offering a solution, a weight for the other side of the scale. The neon sign outside the diner was of a woman leaning back on her palms, knees up, kicking one leg out and bringing it back again. The neon ropes of her hair tumbling down her back, unmoving.

"That's a good idea."

"I've got book club tomorrow night, so if you call me I might not be here."

"Got it."

"But you can text me an update, or call during the day."

"I will."

"Good," she said, and he heard her catch a yawn. She was about to hang up. One of them would say *Okay, then* . . .

"Greg," she said.

"Mm?" he said. He had been about to be the one to say *Okay, then* . . . He watched a tall man in a ball cap get out of an RV next to his, hitching his pants up, walking the way Greg knew he himself would be walking, like his legs were fighting quicksand.

"When you see Marie, just remember you both want the same thing. You both want GJ home. Or found. Just remember that."

"I don't know if that's what Marie wants." He surprised himself by answering this way. Maybe he wanted to argue with Deb about having any kind of common ground with Marie, who often felt less like a fellow parent and more like another child, someone you had to navigate land mines to get near. Or maybe he didn't like the idea that for Deb there were only two options: GJ *home* or

GJ *found*. He tried to soften it, change what he said. "I don't know what she wants. I haven't in years."

"Greg." Deb was using the tone she used when he needed to listen, to gather all parts of himself back from where they'd wandered and report for duty. "You and Marie want the same thing. And you both don't know what to do or if you should even keep fighting for GJ. You're the blind leading the blind, and that's okay. Okay?"

He didn't know what Deb's angle was, suddenly trying to give Marie some recognizable human quality, make them partners in a way they never were. In the early days, when Marie would call, Deb would say, *That witch is on the phone*. But he said, "Okay," and they hung up over a quick *Love ya, Love ya too*, and Greg leaped out of the RV because it seemed less like something a tired old man would do. He zinged his ankles on the landing, had to stomp the sparks out the whole way up to the front door. He tried pushing in but the door wouldn't give, and he stood dazed in the entryway listening to the muffled music, trying to make out the words, thinking about how he hadn't felt nervous about seeing Marie until just now. And then the door opened toward him, revealing the tall man in the ball cap holding two to-go cups of coffee; for a moment Greg wondered if one of them was for him. The man nodded and edged by Greg, the door closing in a cold whoosh of air that smelled of sweat and vanilla. Why was he driving toward that woman? He felt foolish about the door, about the whole trip. He always forgot that sometimes it was a pull, not a push.

Greg showed the man just inside the door his ID, waiting silently as the man studied it under a flashlight and feeling ashamed by the way his hands flapped up to shield his eyes when the man aimed the flashlight at him. A heavy red curtain that was soiled at the bottom hung behind the man, who was as large as Greg and teetering on a stool with uneven metal legs. "Okay," the man finally said, holding Greg's ID out with one hand and using the flashlight to push back the curtain with the other. A wedge of darkness and noise beckoned. "Thank you much," Greg said, in the cheerful twang he used at home, in town getting his hair cut or picking up some firewood. Like this was a normal transaction, like it was a necessary errand on his way to rescuing GJ.

Behind the curtain, down a short hallway, there were two swinging doors: one with bright light behind its porthole window and one with a strobing darkness. Greg looked into the light, saw what appeared to be a family diner. He pushed in for a closer look, thinking maybe he'd just choose this door, maybe he'd get a slice of pie and call it a night, maybe the other door just wasn't for him and that'd be okay. He squinted in the harsh white light, the room smelling of burned coffee and grease, a not entirely unwelcome smell in Greg's opinion. The floor was black and white squares of linoleum; there were round black tables and cracked red booths and a bar with a line of broken stools trying to stand up straight, like men after a bar brawl. A waitress in a powder-blue uniform was shepherding a coffeepot between the only two tables that had customers, two lone men, each hunched over his plate like it needed protecting. The waitress had a high, rigid chest and a pretty but worn face, like it had gone through the wash too many times, and Greg wondered if she had graduated from the dark room to the light. A man behind the counter tossed a dish of fries on the counter and bellowed, "Order up!"

"You seat yourself," the waitress called to him in a scratched monotone that told him she'd been working in loud places for too long. The woman who cut his hair in town had it, always having to yell over the hair dryers when she asked him all the same questions: how was Deb, how was the house, what would he be doing that day? Sometimes circling right back to the beginning, *And now how is Deb?*

"Oh, I'm not hungry," Greg said. "I got that sack of burgers in the car." He had his thumb over his shoulder, pointing back to where he'd come in, like she knew what he was talking about, knew what he drove, knew about the Krystal and GJ and all the rest of it. One of the men turned his head, put his chin on his shoulder to look at Greg without going to much effort. Maybe it was the light, or the quiet, or the smell, but he knew he wouldn't be sitting down to collect himself as he'd originally thought. And maybe it was also that he'd stopped here in the first place, he'd stopped *here*, so early in his trip, which meant he wasn't barreling toward his son, which meant he was quite possibly incapable of facing anything—GJ's disappearance, Marie, fatherhood—and if that was the case then he felt wild with the urge to make this stop count. To see a naked woman, to feel her hair brush his face as carelessly as a bird shitting on his shoulder. As a younger man he'd often taken clients to strip clubs. A boulder of cash in his pocket, ones nesting fives nesting twenties and in the center a few hundreds that only the most dedicated girls would ever catch sight of. Thinking of that, those nights with their own sweat-and-vanilla-scented darkness, Greg felt lighter, like he wasn't presenting the broad expanse of his belly, like he wasn't carrying around a lime-stone slab of torso.

"Are you in the right place?" the waitress asked, setting the cof-feepot down on an empty booth table. "You must want the other door." She wiped her hands on her apron and Greg couldn't help but detect a hint of regret in the gesture, something she tried to hide but couldn't deny, like a sliver of onion in a cookie.

"You got me," he said. "Thank you much." The man who had turned to watch him turned back to his plate, hefting his spoon in his fist like a child. GJ held his utensils the same way. Was it a mark of some kind? *This man will have a hard life.* Deb had tried to break him of the habit, but it never took.

Greg pushed back through the door, into the dark hallway. He heard the man on the stool speaking to someone, another customer perhaps, and pushed through the other door before that person could see him. It was part of the allure of a place like this: no one ever got a good look at anyone or anything. Just glimpses and flashes and the sudden pliant weight of a thigh or a breast or a hip. *No touching, no touching*, the bouncer at one of his old spots used to intone. But there was always touching. Hidden, accidental, on purpose, the bills sliding out of his hands and pockets like he was a flu-struck ATM.

A woman on stage was upside down, her legs in a split, slowly spinning, as bland as a ceiling fan but for the stunned lidless bulging eyes of her breasts, staring out at the men, like, *This?* This *is what you came here for?* A ratty disco ball swayed weakly; a man with wet hair stood in front of the stage, and even from behind Greg could see that the man was openly rubbing the front of his pants. He wore the same kind of gym shorts Greg favored. So this was the kind of place where men showed up in gym shorts, not business suits. Where the bouncer didn't even bother to warn Greg not to touch. A blonde in a neon-green bikini was holding a tray as small as a dinner plate, a tray meant mainly for singles. She came toward Greg, beautiful at first, a specter, and slowly morphing, the closer she got, into a woman who might have some grandchildren, even a great-grandchild or two. Her breasts were hard and looked painfully large. Her skin was tanned the way a hide got tanned and turned into a purse. The blond hair was a wig; she adjusted it like it was a hat, tugging a lock on one side of her face and then tugging a lock on the other side, shifting it into comfort. Why did he notice things like this? Was he the only man in this room who would have noticed? She had worked the wig like she didn't mind him knowing it was a wig. Was that because she truly didn't mind, or because she had gotten used to people not noticing her? He was too sober, maybe that was it. So in that sense this woman was an angel.

"We got two-dollar beers and three-dollar whiskeys. Or you can get a twofer for four dollars." The music was loud and Greg found himself watching her mouth as she spoke. Her teeth glowed white in the darkness. She stared at him, waiting for his order.

Her eyebrows looked drawn on, arched like she was shocked and surprised, *Happy Birthday to me, where am I?*

"I'll take the twofer," he shouted.

She put her hand up to where her ear was under the wig. "What?"

He put his face close, so they were cheek to cheek. The wig smelled brand-new, like plastic, and it seemed to be conducting heat from her scalp. Here was the hair brushing his face, for better or for worse. "The twofer," he said, and dug in his pockets for his change from the stop at the Krystal. He handed her a sweaty five-dollar bill and she plucked it from his hand with the tips of her long nails, like some kind of predatory bird snatching up a rat in its claws. "Keep the change," he shouted, and grinned at her, feeling pleased that he could tip this poor old half-deaf relic twenty percent. If he was tipsy he'd have said something like *You still got it, girl*, glad to flatter and bolster someone older than he was. He knew how good it felt to be flirted with, seen; it was why he stopped for coffee once a week at the place where the college-aged girl called him G and swatted at his arm when he joked with her.

The woman walked behind the bar and assembled his drinks, banged the register and flung the five into the drawer. It was hard to tell but he was pretty sure he could see his whiskey sloshing out of the cup onto the tray as she walked over. She held the tray out; it took Greg a few beats to realize she wasn't going to hand him his drinks, that he'd have to reach out and retrieve them himself. The beer bottle was warm in his hand and the whiskey was in a dented plastic cup. Again he wondered what he was doing, and again he decided he was doing the only thing.

She stood, waiting, and Greg realized she was waiting for a tip. Another tip. He fished out another dollar and placed it on her tray. Out came the claw again, gathering up the bill. She held the tray between her knees as she lifted the wig away from her scalp and pushed the dollar under it. "I'm Pam if you need a refill," she yelled, readjusting her wig again, and then walked over to serve other men. Greg watched the silly waggle of her rear, its flesh all give. Deb wore underwear to conceal, to protect, to hide. She knew her strengths and she knew her weaknesses. The only time he glimpsed her ass these days was in the shower, behind the new glass doors they'd had put in. Clenched and puckered like a dog with its tail between its legs. Still, it thrilled him to see it, the naked ass of the woman he loved. He did not thrill at the sight of Pam's.

He sat in a chair to the left of the stage. There was a new woman up there now, flat on her back kicking her legs in the air, displaying the swollen folds of her vagina, the raisin eye of her asshole. Not a hair to be seen. All those layers of flesh, like a complicated pastry. The man with the wet hair was still up there, but now Greg could see he had his hand *in* his shorts. He almost had the answer, right then, the answer to why he'd come, and he pictured taking a running start, sliding to home, landing inside this woman, *safe!* Everyone in this room doing away with any pretense, letting it all hang out there, wig and scars and tortured hard-ons. Calling a spade a spade. He could be who he was and no one would give a shit. He took the whiskey all in one gulp, opening his throat to let it slide down. The beer was like swallowing his own warm spit, but it felt necessary to continue drinking. Sometimes drinking was necessary. GJ had learned that, too. Sometimes it wasn't. GJ had ignored that part. The woman rolled to her side and spun like a compass going haywire. It had to be difficult, thinking of new moves, moves that would set you apart from the other girls, ways to showcase your body, ways to distract yourself. Greg threw his last single onto the stage. He had a twenty left and that was it. As if she could sense it, could feel that twenty burning his pocket all up, like his dick had risen up and pointed right at it, another woman in a bikini appeared. No tray, no wig as far as he could tell. He could smell sex on her, that smell like saliva and salt and the wetness Greg could never help but mention in the heat of the moment.

"Do you want to come with me?" she asked. She put both hands on his neck, cradling him. One of her breasts was larger than the other and the smaller one looked like it had been pummeled with a meat mallet. "It's fifty."

Greg had never gone with one of the women before, at the other clubs; he'd seen clients be led into curtained rooms and come out with exhausted faces and wet lips; he'd gone out the back exit once and seen his colleague being pinned to a wall with one red-nailed hand while the other pumped at his crotch like a piston. His partner had nodded the way they did passing each other in the hall at work, then closed his eyes.

The music was loud, so loud that he felt like it might all be in his head, just a crush of noise out of which he tried to find the words. In truth he had always regretted not being the one to go behind the curtain, to unzip before a stranger and lean back. And back then the woman wouldn't have had to reach under the hull of his belly to find his prick. Now all he had to offer was a hard-on of bodily girth, the swollen fatness of him. He and Deb had sex on special occasions only. She never took him in hand, never led him in. It was up to him to pump the dime-sized portion of lube, to push in, to get it over with. In a way that felt even more filthy than having sex with a wife was supposed to feel, both of them just doing it as a favor to the other. Deb patting his back when it was all said and done, polite and firm as always; she'd be patting the back of the angel of death when her time came.

But what did he expect? They were old and getting older.

"I only have twenty," he shouted to the woman before him, hating himself, but relieved to have an excuse all the same.

She shrugged, let go of his neck, and stepped back. "Twenty'll buy you a lap dance," she said, and held out her hand. She said it halfheartedly, as if Greg was her last hope. One of the narrow triangles of her bikini top had shifted, and from where Greg sat it appeared she was missing a nipple, and was that a scar? He couldn't tear his eyes away.

"You like that?" She looked down at the smoothness that should have been nipple. "That's road burn, Daddy. Motorcycle accident. You can touch for five." She took the beer from his hand, raised it up, and licked its mouth slowly with her tongue before handing it back. He suddenly thought of the waitress behind the door of light; had she ever lifted a coffee cup and licked it like that?

"No," he said, louder than he wanted to. The music was in between songs and the dancer onstage looked over at him as she bent to collect her dollars. "I mean, no thank you," he said to the woman in the bikini. He reached out and patted her arm.

"Now you owe me five," she said. She shifted the top back into place, crossed her arms over her ribs. The man with the wet hair was watching now; the dancer lingering onstage, boldly staring at Greg.

Greg held out the twenty. "I'll need change," he said. Again the feeling of shame, of foolishness. Like he was being burned from the toes up, burned alive by a creeping flame that was only ever warm. Asking for change from a stripper. Standing in a strip club in his open sandals and slightly nicer pair of gym shorts and his penis nestled like something exhausted, something only ever warm. With a jolt, he remembered taking GJ to a strip club on his eighteenth birthday. Had wanted to do something unexpected, shocking. Had wanted to seem as young as GJ, maybe. On his own eighteenth birthday his mother had given him a suitcase. He had wanted to show the boy his view of the world. In truth he was the kind of father who expected GJ to make mistakes, but only all the same mistakes he himself had made. And he had never told the boy that being happy wasn't the point. Who was happy? When had he been happy? That day on the library steps. It came to him before he could stop it. That day on the library steps, he'd been happy. Was it worth what came after? GJ had wanted to leave after seeing the first dancer, but Greg pulled him into the bathroom, let him sip from his drink until he felt better about staying. Greg was older now; his son had been an adult for years. He could see how he'd been trying to show the boy he'd been as a teenager what life could be. He could see how he'd only ever seen GJ as a mirror, not a window. These moments came to him more and more, especially after he retired. These lists of failures. He had time to reflect. What was the point? He could dole apologies out upon GJ one by one, like Band-Aids, like dollar bills. But the damage had been done. Too much road burn. They were both smooth and swollen and beyond themselves. Where was GJ? He had been worried about the boy for almost thirty years. When would it end? Where the fuck was he?

The woman in the bikini had gone and come back. "Here's your change," she yelled, holding a fan of ones out to him. A simple business transaction for her, nothing more. She was cutting her eyes over to a new customer; Greg was surprised to see that it was a woman, a large woman in a Hawaiian shirt leaning back in her chair looking like she came here all the time. He took his money and the woman in the bikini walked quickly away, toward this new customer, to cradle the woman's neck in her hands as she'd cradled his. As he left he saw the woman in the bikini leading the

other woman by the hand, toward the back where it was too dark
to see if there were curtains or doors or just an open dark space
where they could conduct their business. So sometimes it *was* better for everyone if he just left. *Ha.* He'd have to remember to tell
that one to . . . who? Maybe he'd stop by the bar on the way out.
Just a shot or two.

And then he was in the small hallway again, between the two
doors. His shin throbbed; had he tripped and hit it on something?
He was sweating. The hallway was too narrow; he was too big. His
belly burned from something he ate or drank. Or both. He looked
into the light but he couldn't see the waitress, and one of the customers had left, so now it was just the one. If he died and these
were the two doors he had to choose from, the one in the light
definitely seemed more like hell, that stillness and quiet, than the
one in the dark.

"Good night," he said to the bouncer, who did not return the
sentiment.

He walked quickly across the parking lot to the RV. His sandals
slapped the asphalt; his heart thudded heavily. He heaved himself
into the RV. He was starting to feel afraid he'd pull it onto its side,
that he was heavier than the vehicle. He had to crouch around
inside like a teddy bear in a dollhouse, but he managed to climb
up into the loft bed above the front seats. Didn't even take his
shoes off—he'd have to bow his body, reach his toes, and that was
out of the question. He'd forgotten a pillow and a blanket but he
could stop for those the following day. He was shocked, disappointed even, that it was only just past eleven o'clock. Well, if there
was anything he was good at, it was stalling.

Marie got pregnant three months in. *I didn't* get *pregnant*, she would say, years later. *It takes two to tango.* They were both starved, bingeing, desperate for any opportunity to meet up. Greg's roommate leaving for class meant two whole hours to themselves; sometimes Marie borrowed a friend's car and they would end up parked by the Dumpsters behind the grocery store, often barely making it into the backseat. It was like Greg's penis had becoming a divining rod and Marie was a lake in the desert. They both confessed to feeling pain, actual physical pain, when they weren't joined together, sloppily moving and repositioning and laughing until it wasn't funny anymore. And staying joined even when it was over, talking about everyday things, how Marie's roommate snored or how Greg had taken a second shift on the weekends. The best times were when they couldn't make any noise; when they were in his dorm room with the walls as thin as newspaper or the one afternoon when they succumbed to the silent shelves in an abandoned aisle in the library. Staring into each other's eyes, gasping and whispering about how it felt so good, so good, so good. Sometimes they used a condom, but only sometimes. He felt like he'd found it, the secret to a happy life: all he had to do was give in. All he had to do was get away from his mother, far away from her edicts on propriety and manners and how a woman could only love a man who could provide. He felt like he'd won a small private war inside himself. He couldn't wait to bring Marie home, to see his mother taking her in, assessing the loose and frizzy hair, the open, makeupless face, the *jeans*. Marie didn't smoke and she didn't care what she looked like. They had met on the common one early morning, before the whole world was awake, and she'd shocked him when he'd kissed her and tasted the thick brackish saliva of sleep. He'd brushed his teeth and she had not, and she had kissed him openly and with relish. That's when he told her he loved her, the sour smell from her mouth on his lips, the words feeling strange and scripted but all he could think of to say.

And then Marie told him she was pregnant. They were in her friend's car, which she'd borrowed less and less lately, now that they'd gotten good at sneaking into each other's dorm room or going to the same parties and locking themselves in someone's bedroom. Greg felt excited about the car, like it was an old friend, but Marie had pulled into a gas station and parked. She unbuckled her seat belt and turned to him and for a fleeting moment Greg felt alarmed that she'd want to have sex in the open, families driving in and out and maybe even some of their friends. But no: "I'm pregnant," she said. He giggled; it was a habit of his even when dealing with the disappointment or anger of his mother. He knew he shouldn't laugh and so he did laugh.

"I'm not kidding," she said.

He knew she wasn't; he remembered all the times they hadn't worn a condom, all the times he'd let go inside her because it felt so good, so good. Of course she was pregnant. She still hadn't said she loved him, but Greg couldn't stop telling her; it often felt like the only thing he had to say to her.

He put a hand out to touch her where the baby was. "Okay," he said.

"Don't do that," she said. She had never told him not to touch her. He'd put his fingers and tongue everywhere he could think to put them and she had never balked. But now she pushed his hand away; she pushed his hand away from his own child.

He felt ashamed, like he'd done the wrong thing. "Is it mine?" he asked. He had wanted her to feel the same shame; it was right out of his mother's playbook, and he instantly regretted it. "I'm joking," he said, but they both knew he wasn't.

"I don't know about keeping it," she said. They were throwing darts at each other now. He wanted to ask her to back out of the parking space, keep backing out, reverse the entire afternoon. He watched a child using a rag to wash the windshield of his mother's car, the windshield getting more and more fogged with grease; nobody was making anything any better.

"Marry me," he said. "Marie me." Again he giggled, but he was forcing it now, attempting his own peeling tires. He had thought of asking her to marry him more than once. If they lived in the same house, they'd never have to leave each other, could sleep all night joined at the crotch; he could wake up inside her. And now they could keep the child and raise it.

She was pinching bits of vinyl from the steering wheel, rolling them between her fingers, placing them in the ashtray. "Okay," she said.

He had felt more afraid of her saying no than of her saying yes, of what saying yes meant. Looking back, after all that had happened, Greg often wondered if she had orchestrated the whole thing. The way she'd said *Okay*. Like it was a given, like she was just waiting for him to assume it'd been his idea. But he had filled her with himself, it had taken two to tango.

But in the car on that hot day, her *Okay* thrilled him. Now they were really in it together; he had chosen his partner and the life before him. "Okay," he said, as if they'd settled on a place for lunch. They drove back to campus, snuck into her room, and had celebratory sex on the floor by her desk, her in his lap, eye to eye, both coming quickly, thankfully for Greg, whose ass burned as it moved against the rough carpet. She had called him *husband*, and he had let go, no need to worry about pulling out now since it was already too late. They married the following month in the chapel on campus, Marie walking toward him in a yellow dress and him without a suit coat; it was hot and they were broke. Greg's mother sent a funeral wreath in her absence; she claimed it was a mix-up and she'd meant to send a flowering plant for them to nourish in their new home and life together. But it seemed like a curse she'd placed upon them: Marie bled the next morning. Just as he'd hoped, they'd gone to bed joined, but they had woken up apart, in a hot puddle of blood that smelled alive. They hadn't bothered to put sheets on the bed yet, and the mattress absorbed the blood and it dried over time into a jagged brown stain that they tried to ignore each time they changed the sheets. Marie bled their child out in their first week of marriage, both of them stunned and exhausted, drinking beer after beer, sitting apart among their boxes of books and cracked dishes in the student apartment they'd rented. He hadn't truly faced the idea of fatherhood yet. The focus had been on getting married, moving in. His grief felt diluted, harmless, easily dissolved. For Marie, the miscarriage was a betrayal of her body, and of fate itself. Something she hadn't overcome, hadn't even seen coming.

"A lot of women miscarry," she said once, shaking her head, as if all of them were stupid for even trying. Or, "You know, we don't have to stay married now." He had written that off as part of the unavoidable rage the loss was pumping into her body, but in the end perhaps she had been right. After the miscarriage they were just two young people who'd gotten married too quickly, who refused to admit it had been a mistake, that they should call it and start over.

But they did stay together, telling themselves it was impossible to break the lease of their student apartment, and then helping each other finish school, first Greg and then Marie, and then staying together because their friends were now marrying and it was easier to be taken by the current. But Marie began taking birth control, never forgetting a dose, not wanting to allow her body to take over her life ever again. At night they still reached for each other, still strangers in so many ways, and that was what they craved most of all: the anonymity of the dark, the shock of touch. Her chilly hands pushing him deeper and deeper in. The ability to make this person, this near stranger, cry out, beg for more; the ability to remain unknown, the ability to still feel young, at least in the dark. It was the power each held over the other, night after night, year after year: we have failed, we are failing.

It was raining when he woke up. The loft bed might have been comfortable if Greg had been six inches shorter and a hundred pounds lighter, but he'd slept anyway, hard, waking up curled like a boy asleep under a tree. He couldn't move his feet like usual; they felt strapped, and when he shot up to have a look he bonked his head on the loft ceiling. He bellowed, looking for something to throw, or hit, but there was nothing. He was just a fat old man yelling inside his rented RV. His neck ached. It hurt to turn his head. His feet were still in his sandals; now it all made sense. The wad of fifteen singles from the woman in the bikini felt embedded in his thigh. He heard trucks pulling in and out of the parking lot around him, honking to each other. He climbed down from the loft. For what felt like the millionth time in his life, he cursed his heft, his uncontrollable hunger, his helpless anchored body, even as his mouth got wet over a whiff of bacon and eggs and coffee from the diner.

Behind a slim door wedged next to the kitchenette, a tall, narrow canister housed the toilet and shower. The toilet had a white plastic seat that hid what looked like an endless cavern to Greg, and almost directly above that was the removable showerhead, its nozzle bearded with calcification. It amazed Greg, how people made do. He could sit on the toilet and wash himself if he was in a rush and needed to multitask. He laughed at the thought. He felt the same way he did when he first laid eyes on his dorm room and saw that his and his roommate's twin beds were arm's length apart. It felt like a novelty, something he didn't have to take seriously.

He pulled the navy accordion blinds down on the big window that faced the parking lot and undressed, using his toes to work the sandals off his swollen feet, since bending down in the RV's small living area felt out of the question. His body filled the canister; his shoulders brushed the cheap plastic walls. He turned right and left, trying to find the sweet spot, like his corpse was spinning in an ill-fitting coffin. He would never be able to close the pantry door behind him. He ended up with one foot planted just outside the shower, which allowed most of his body to get wet, and then he turned and planted the other foot outside the shower to get the remaining parts of his body. The RV had come with a small pat of soap in paper wrapping that claimed its scent was Forest Floor but actually smelled like nothing at all. He used that to lather his hair and chest, armpits and lower region before it slipped from his fingers and skidded out of the shower altogether. Deb never nagged him about his weight, but sometimes he felt like she challenged him in other ways. *They call it a compact*, she'd said about the RV. Might as well have said, *Good luck, fatty.* How much had he weighed the last time he saw Marie? He wasn't wearing gym shorts so much back then. He wasn't retired either. Sometimes he wanted to ask GJ who was the worse parent, him or Marie. He used to feel desperate for leverage over her, but he hadn't felt that way in years, now that they didn't speak. But here he was, his ass hanging out of a lipstick-sized shower in the parking lot of a strip club he'd stopped at so he wouldn't have to keep driving toward her. He needed her to be fat, too. *You both want the same thing,* Deb said.

He used the showerhead to rinse himself as best he could, but the soap left a slippery film behind no matter how much he ran the water over his skin. The water seemed to be getting weaker, too, like it was losing heart. He'd forgotten to bring towels, so he dried himself with the shirt he'd been wearing the day before and dressed in the khakis and short-sleeved button-down he'd brought for occasions when gym shorts weren't appropriate. He couldn't decide what made him look larger, tucking the shirt in or leaving it out, and finally decided leaving it out at least allowed him the dignity of hiding the feminine paunch, like the bottom half of a peach, that belted pants seemed to showcase whenever he wore them.

The sack of burgers smelled sour, and Greg ran through the rain to throw them in the trash can outside the diner. He had packed only his sandals; his feet and the cuffs of his pants were now soggy and chilled, and it was enough to convince him that he didn't want to go back into the diner and get a bite. He ran back through the rain to the RV. He sat sideways in the dinette, its chipped table pushing into his ribs. He was thankful for the noise of the trucks. He leaned over and folded back the navy blind to watch them heave themselves into and out of the parking spots, honking hellos and goodbyes, leviathans of the rain in this middle of nowhere. He folded his gym shorts and placed them in his duffel, draped the shirt he'd used as a towel over the back of the passenger seat to dry. He needed to stop for towels, a pillow, a blanket, and coffee, but that was it. There wasn't a single other thing to do but drive until he was pulling in to the parking lot of Marie's condo.

As he slid in, he was pleased all over again with the softness of the driver's seat. Its plushness, its wideness. A rare place where he fit just fine. He wondered why he hadn't slept in it the night before. As he heaved his own leviathan out of its space he honked a goodbye, the trucks honking back, and he felt a joy so sudden and sharp in his sinuses that he mistook it for grief and cried for four whole exits, when he got off at the promise of a Walgreens.

The rain stopped after he'd driven a few hours, the sky going from gray to a colorless haze, like it hadn't made up its mind yet. He held an open box of Poppycock in his lap; he'd gotten to the dregs already. It felt good to chew, to have handful after handful to look forward to, his tongue mining out bits of salty and sweet that he could re-enjoy, washing it all down with a lukewarm Yoo-hoo. He had crossed the Florida state line fifty miles back. His clothes felt damp and wrinkled, formed to his body like strips of papier-mâché. He'd tried to call Deb, his hands oily from the popcorn, but she hadn't picked up. He dialed GJ again, the hundredth time, the hundredth hundredth time, but it didn't even ring. The same annoyed woman's voice, the same disappointed *The number you have dialed* . . . GJ's phone was often turned off, lost, traded. It didn't alarm Greg not to be able to get him on the phone. It didn't alarm him that GJ was out of pocket. Taken apart, each piece of evidence wasn't damning, wasn't out of the ordinary, he reminded himself often. For a while Greg had watched a show on cable about addicts and their families, had become entranced by the pain, the crying, the terrible things the cameras caught the addicts doing. One man took the cameras on a tour of all the houses he'd broken into; on another episode, a woman with a bald head rolled up her sleeve to reveal what looked to Greg like someone had piled mud in the crook of her elbow. *I blew a vein and it got infected*, she said, smiling into the camera, sheepish and unconcerned. The addicts often disappeared, came back, disappeared again, showing up asking for money or calling from the hospital or somewhere else. Greg knew an addict's life was a selfish one. The families used that word again and again. *You're selfish. Stop being selfish. We want you around.* He wished for a camera crew, for an addiction expert in a sweater vest who could come along and show him a script for how it was going to play out. Many of the addicts had been abused, or their parents had been neglectful, or they themselves had been addicts. Their families cried for all the mistakes they'd made, for all the time they'd lost. It felt good to cry with the families, to nod, to try not to make any noise even though his mouth was open, even though Deb was off somewhere and couldn't hear him anyway. Most of the addicts went to the rehab the expert offered to them; most of those ended up using again a short time after being released.

Greg hadn't considered what he'd do if, when, he found GJ holed up in a girlfriend's house or in jail, perfectly fine and sheepish like always. He'd be angry. He'd let himself be angry. He'd yell and yell. It felt like a gift, this possibility that GJ was just being an asshole again.

He saw a hitchhiker up ahead, standing on the shoulder, just a black shape with its arm out. Greg couldn't see a car nearby, he didn't think this man had been stranded by a flat tire or an overheated engine. As he got closer he saw that the man was wearing tattered clothes and a backpack, a black-and-red-and-green beanie on his head. Holding his arm out like he was hailing a taxi. And even as Greg thought, *What a dumbass, thinking he can look like that and get a ride*, he slowed the RV and pulled onto the shoulder fifty yards from the man, who was actually closer in age to a kid. He jogged to the passenger-side window and Greg leaned over and pushed the button, bringing the window down halfway.

"Hey," the kid said, smiling. Greg saw now that he was no more than college-aged. His teeth were mostly white and his eyes were clear.

"You trying to get a ride?" Greg asked. "I haven't seen a hitch-hiker in years."

"Looking to get to Tampa," he said. "There's a concert I'm try-ing to get to." He looked at Greg, still smiling, his hand on the window and the other hand holding the strap of his backpack.

Greg had slowed and pulled over, he realized, partly in the spirit of the trip, the one that let him meander and reflect and that would lead him directly to his son. A hero's journey. But seeing the man up close, hearing his voice, he realized he'd also slowed hoping the man would be GJ. Believing it was him because stranger things have happened and because he was looking for GJ, that was the sole purpose of barreling down the highway toward his ex-wife in a compact RV, and if you look for something it eventually turns up in the damnedest place, usually right where you've already looked a hundred times, a hundred hundred times. Was anyone looking for this man? Was he really going to a concert in Tampa? Had GJ tried hitchhiking; was he a hit-and-run or a prisoner or a corpse robbed of its drugs and the watch he'd received from Greg, which he'd never pawned, not yet?

"Call your father," Greg said. He held out his oily phone.

"What, man?" The kid hitched his backpack higher on his shoulder, put his hand up to his ear. His smile was losing steam.

"I think you should call your father and check in," Greg said. He leaned over, crushing the box of Poppycock under his belly, and tapped the phone on the kid's knuckles.

It was what he wished someone would do for him. Someone offer GJ a phone; tell him what to do. *Call your father. Stop hiding. Get out of the road.* Camera crew and script.

"No thanks, man," the kid said. He backed away from the RV. "I'll find another ride." He had his hands up as if the phone Greg held out was a gun. Greg still paid GJ's phone bill. He wanted his son to have a phone to call and be called. But GJ had always treated it like a burden, something silly that only his dad and no one else in the world cared about. *It's just a phone, Dad.*

"It's just a phone," he called out to the kid, who kept his hands up and shook his head. Greg put the phone in a cup holder so the kid would relax. "Do you know someone named GJ?" he called. GJ went to concerts when he was younger, at first because he liked music and then because he was selling drugs, which Greg found out after GJ had been arrested at a concert in the park.

"DJ?"

"G. GJ," Greg said. "Gregory Junior." Again came the surprise grief, his eyes flooding and spilling down his cheeks. "I'm sorry," he said, his voice raw. "Been driving a lot. I'm just tired."

The kid walked closer, put his hand back on the window. "I don't know him," he said. "I'm going to walk up a little bit so I can keep trying to find a ride, but I think you should just park here for a while. Get yourself together." The kid held his hand up in a wave and jogged away.

Greg let the tears come, flowing out like he'd been tapped.

His throat ached. He eased the RV back onto the highway. When he passed the kid, he felt a sudden embarrassed rage. That kid playing at being a loner, playing at being open to the world, *Hey, man, check out this hat, check out the dirt in my nails.* Greg hadn't even offered the boy a ride; all he'd done was show his hand. The boy couldn't deal. His parents probably knew right where he was; had probably dropped him off at the highway exit and waved good-bye. GJ didn't even like being dropped off at school. *I want to stay with you.* And Greg just answering, *You'll be fine,* his mother's words. One time even rolling the window up, GJ snatching his hand away so it wouldn't get crushed. He was trying to prepare the boy for the day that he'd be dropped off for good, the day he became an adult. He was trying to prepare the boy for heartache and drudgery and disappointment. Smooth out his edges. A smooth stone skips easily over the water; GJ went straight to the bottom, *I want to stay with you,* Greg pivoting and flicking his wrist and letting the boy go, *plonk.*

He glanced in the rearview, but the kid was gone.

And then he was only fourteen exits from Marie. He drove slowly, coasting in the right lane, counting them down as he went. *I know why you married her,* Marie had said one afternoon when he and Deb were dropping GJ off after a weekend together. Deb had stayed in the car, lifted a hand in a bland, placid wave. Marie returned the same nothing wave. *She's perfect for you, you know,* she'd said. *Because it's like you can be alone without being lonely.* Then she'd smiled at him like they were in on the joke, and closed the door. Heading back to the car he'd smiled to himself, and then at Deb. Marie was right, and what was wrong with that? But it stayed with him, and it began to molder and stink, and after a while he could see what Marie truly meant. Deb accepted him for who he was, big body and all, end of story, a never-ending ending.

Companionship was what it could be called. Greg shook himself. Marie was always finding a way in, making him feel doubtful. He had led a peaceful existence with Deb for many years. It was time to pull off now, time for the game face he'd have to put on to face Marie. There were no more exits to go.

He had glimpsed bits of Florida from the highway, tall gas-station signs and a gluttony of palm trees and the heat coming in through the windows despite the constant exhale of air-conditioning through the vents in the RV, heat that made seeing drivers in their bathing suits or shirtless men riding shotgun taking polite swigs of beer seem like no big deal. Greg had forgotten how the heat made shorts a necessity, how flip-flops and tank tops were part of the uniform, if you could stand to wear that many items of clothing. If you cropped the picture just so, you could get a portrait of nature, a foreign, mean, insect-laden, sun-beaten, green slice of the outdoors. "Ponce de Leon," he said to himself, driving along the road he took after leaving the highway, the one that shot east and west in a near-perfect straight line, the one that would take him ever closer to Marie's condo. Ponce de Leon, Florida's first explorer. GJ had learned that in school, had loved to say the man's name. Ponce de Leon named Florida, which means "place of flowers." Now it could be known as "place of Circle Ks," "place of rednecks," "place of sprawl." If you pulled back to capture a wider view, that's when you got a better picture. Apartment complexes in tans and beiges; tile-roofed strip malls; brown-water beaches; textured and freckled and crisped skin. Greg had lived in places where you could get by without air-conditioning, where it was a badge of honor to go without, but it had never been that way here. People loved to go into the shopping malls and movie theaters and Chili's and Olive Garden because it was guaranteed to be ice cold inside, an escape from the squinting and sweating and constant nuisance of fabric against your body.

Greg hadn't been overweight when he'd lived in Florida, not all that much, anyway. It was a new sensation, that extra weight of sweat pulling his shirt closer, like a room with collapsing walls. He felt betrayed by his driver's seat, which seemed also to be sucking him deeper in, his ass seeping into his khakis, every part of him melting but not getting any smaller. He had gotten used to it in the fifteen years he'd lived in central Florida, his blood had adapted to the constant heat; but once he left, all of that had faded away. Coming back to visit GJ, he'd feel himself dissolving again, his body cooked, his face exhausted from baring his teeth to squint his eyes, even wearing sunglasses.

There were beautiful parts of it, too: old brick roads and older stucco homes and shady trees dripping moss; quiet lakes and endless green and candy-blue swimming pools and yes, the palm trees. Greg had never gotten over the palm trees. They had one in the yard out front of the house they lived in—he, Marie, and GJ—but they were everywhere, even inside shopping malls. The cold and snow offered its own harsh unrelenting bullshit, its layers of clothing and short, gray days, its long nights, its ice and salt. But it seemed more natural to Greg, to have the seasons change, to watch everything die and be buried, gone gone gone, and then the soggy resurrection of spring, the smell of black mud and the sight of green sprouting out of a melting patch of gray. In Florida it was an everlasting summer, a relentless oven. The first thing you noticed about a person was how he kept his feet, which seemed childish to Greg when he lived there, but it was another thing he missed, along with the palm trees. He wore sandals when he could now; he kept his feet as tidy as he could, trimming the nails with Deb's nail scissors and sometimes using a Band-Aid to hide a small bit of fungus.

Marie lived in a development with manufactured rolling hills, sodded of course, that encircled three short rows of condominiums, four stories high and three units deep. Marie had a view of the parking lot, something the developers did their best to minimize with palm trees and shrubbery and ornate iron grating. It was either that or a view of the retention pond, which wouldn't have been so bad if the developers hadn't quickly placed a chain-link fence around it when residents complained that small children could wander down to get a better look at the filthy ducks splashing around in it, fall in, and . . . Marie had told GJ all of this, and GJ had recounted it to Greg, near-breathless with excitement to be included in the discussions of which condo to choose: front, middle, or back? That was when Greg lived in his apartment, a one-bedroom shithole that did its best to rise above its class in life (faux-granite countertops; glass doors in the shower; textured ceilings that the leasing agent pointed to the way a fraudulent jeweler might gesture to a cubic zirconium).

The condo was in a gated community, but Greg was able to follow a Hummer in, which felt like a miracle. It was Saturday, but he suddenly realized that he had no idea if she'd be home.

Greg sometimes thought of it as *his* condo, since surely she'd purchased it with the money from the divorce, but pulling in, he felt afraid. This was her turf. All of Florida was her turf, the whole state feeling off-limits to him, blacked out, redacted. Every resident in the complex might be watching him; who drove a Hummer unless you were someone looking for a fight? But the Hummer pulled up to the mailboxes and a thin woman in bright orange flip-flops got out, holding up her keys in a wave. Greg waved back and drove past.

Up close, the iron grating of the covered parking looked old and rusted. There were yellow patches in the green rolling hills, and more than one car had a serious dent in it. The palm trees wore shaggy skirts of their own dead fronds. It wasn't there yet, but the place was going to shit. Marie should get out while she could; he started having the conversation in his head, the one where he asked her what her plans were and then she asked him just why he cared, and there in the RV, with his gut shellacked to his shirt by a slime of sweat, he had to agree that the Marie in his head had a point. He didn't care. Twenty minutes, tops. In, out. *Where's GJ? Where's GJ? Where is our son?* Answer, no answer, he'd be back in the RV in twenty.

He turned down her row of parking. There was nowhere to put the RV. If he pulled in between the parking-space lines, half of his compact RV would be sitting in the narrow roadway. And he'd never make it under the covered parking. Instead he pulled the RV parallel to the curb, taking up three or four spaces. If Marie was looking out her window she'd definitely see him coming, so he waited on the other side of the RV for a few minutes, letting the blood flow back to his legs, hoping the weak breeze might dry some of the sweat. His toes looked pale, stunned, like grubworms under a flashlight. He walked around the front of the RV, his heart pounding. He had made it his life's mission to keep contact with this woman down to almost nothing. Would she laugh at him? Put her hand over her mouth and look at him with amused and pitying eyes? He could take it. He had to take it. In, out.

He tripped on a divot of asphalt and fell to his knee, his sandal bending under his foot and zings of pain shooting up his thigh. He was holding himself up by his fingertips. He pushed himself to standing and kept walking, but there was Marie. Shoulder-length black hair behind her ears, the same kind of flowery blouse she always favored, shapeless and flowing, cropped khaki pants, crossed arms.

"Do you have GJ?" she called. And then, "Oh, Christ, your knee is bleeding." Greg looked down and saw a tear in his pants, a dark red gash of blood. "I have stuff inside to clean that up."

He hadn't thought to buy Band-Aids or Neosporin at the Walgreens, and Marie was the type to put a poultice of herbs on a gunshot wound. "It's no big deal," he said. He hadn't planned out what he'd say to her when he first saw her, but *It's no big deal* would not have been high on the list.

"I have real stuff," she said. She turned and walked toward her open door, and Greg saw that she had a hitch in her step, like her hips were too tight. Like she was old. She wasn't fat, but she was fatter than she had been, like she'd been fluffed. She was wearing orthopedic sandals, shoes that Deb called *old lady shoes*. Deb was younger than they were; she didn't understand. Yet. He followed Marie, turning to look down the dark hallway to the RV. *In and out*, he told himself. *In and out*, the RV answered back.

Marie stood at her door, waiting for him to go in first. "Go on in," she said. "Wait for me on the couch." His knee felt hot with pain. She had decorated in earth tones. *Earth tones*, another phrase she favored. Deb liked whites and grays. Marie's couch was a deep red; a fat spray of woodsy greens decorated her coffee table; a tapestry was mounted on the wall behind the television, woven browns and reds, like an ode to shit and blood. He hated it; it was like something you'd see on TV in a college dorm. None of it calming; all of it shouting, hollering, screeching. When he sat on the couch it made a *whump* noise. It was as plush as the RV's driver's seat, and he felt himself sinking, losing control of his posture, so he sat forward, his elbows on his splayed knees.

"I saw you pull up," Marie called from the bathroom, which had been painted a deep clay orange, if Greg remembered correctly. "I was coming out to yell that you can't park like that." She walked into the room holding a bag of cotton balls and hydrogen peroxide. "Sometimes the mouthbreathers around here have family come stay and tell them to park their trucks and vans and RVs in the way back." She bit off a corner of the bag and took out a handful of cotton balls, which she doused with the peroxide. "Like because we're back here we won't care." She waited, bent over him, holding the cotton poised just above his knee. "You're going to have to pull your pants up or down."

She was still attractive, Greg could see now. Her eyes were still jet black, her lips wrinkled but full. She still stared full on into his eyes; she'd never stopped doing that, even when it was at its ugliest between them. It was unnerving but hard to look away. Push, pull. He reached down and ripped the hole in his pants wider. "There," he said. "Now I don't have to do either."

She held the cold cotton to his knee. The fizzing felt like a million tiny teeth eating away at his leg, moving in for his bone. "I've never seen you fall before," she said. "Here." She gestured for him to take over holding the cotton. She sat next to him on the couch, no *whump* for her. "So GJ isn't with you, then?"

"No," he said. "I came here to look for him." Saying it out

loud to Marie felt ridiculous. *Idiotic*, a word GJ loved as a teen-ager. A tear of peroxide slid down his shin.

"He's not here," she said. She took the cotton from him and placed it on her coffee table; she'd never cared about keeping furniture in good condition. "I told you over the phone that I don't know where he is. You think I wouldn't call you if that had changed?"

"I had to do something," he said. "He's been gone three weeks."

"I know that," she said. She was dousing more cotton balls. "I know how long my son has been missing."

"Did you file a police report yet?"

"Did you?"

"No. I figured, what if—"

"What if the police find him and he's doing something that could get him arrested again," Marie said. She handed him the new batch of cotton and started unpeeling a Band-Aid. She still had fake nails, something she'd started doing after they divorced, fat white tips that looked like she dipped her fingers in Wite-Out. *She's trying to be young*, GJ said once. They were at Mick's, both craning their necks up at a golf tournament neither cared about. Greg had asked about Marie, something he did to make GJ feel like he still cared, but also because it allowed him to keep tabs on her without having to talk to her. *She's fine. She got a lot of new clothes. Did her nails. She's trying to be young.* Greg laughed to show GJ that this was a laughable, silly thing, but he had recently bought silk undershorts for the same reason he imagined Marie was making herself over. Marriage froze them in time, forever young inside but aging on the outside. Divorce unfroze them, and there was so much catching up to do.

"That's part of it," Greg said. He took the bandage from her and stuck it to his wet knee, could already feel it sliding off.

"I get it," Marie said. "Any move you make feels too final, too *real*." *Too real*. Marie always wanting to proclaim something as too real or unreal. "He's been gone longer than ever, Gregory."

This had been exactly what he'd been trying to say to her just moments ago, and she'd snapped at him. Now it was supposed to be some revelation?

"I know how long my son has been missing," he said. She laughed, a single dry *ha* that he felt sure she believed made her seem superior. On the reading chair behind her, a gray cat suddenly appeared, its tail like a brushstroke come alive, fluid and undulating, its green eyes both alarmed and disgusted at this fat sweaty oaf sitting on the couch. Greg's throat prickled, as if someone had blown the puff of a dandelion back there, each seed carrying a bloom of itch.

"What do you want to do," Marie asked, and there didn't seem to be a question mark at the end of the sentence. It was a statement, bored and flat. *What do you want to do*. Greg started counting all the tiles he could see, that old habit rearing up whenever he felt cornered. He stopped himself after thirteen tiles, but he wanted to roll up the rug, push back the love seat, push it onto the tiny porch if it would fit among all the creeping vines and potted whatevers and carpet of dead leaves, so he could keep counting. The cat poured off the chair and began plucking at the rug with its paws. *Making biscuits*. Who called it that? Deb, who loved cats. So she had that in common with Marie. Greg sneezed, holding the crumpled Band-Aid wrapper up to catch the shout of air and spit. He had no idea what he wanted to do. This had been his destination, and now he was here, and now it was dissolving, no longer. He shrugged, because it was what GJ would have done. What are you doing with your life? *Shrug*. Don't you want to live? *Shrug*. Where are you? *Shrug*.

"We could look for him in places he used to go," Marie said. She got up and sat in the chair the cat had vacated. Greg wondered if he smelled, if the RV's essence had invaded his pores, gotten muddled in his sweat and fear and love of meat. But likely she just didn't want to sit next to her ex-husband, the father of her fucked-up son, this fat lump who shrugged in the face of the unknown.

"I googled him the other night," she said. "I found his arrest records, all stuff we knew about. I found that blog he had back in high school, too. No new posts. And I found this other guy with his name, this man who lives in Idaho with his wife and four children. He's the principal of an elementary school out there. He loves the television show *Law and Order*. His favorite band is Metallica. One of his daughters' names is Hailey. I found all that about this other Greg, even his address and phone number. We could drive to his house right now. I couldn't stop learning about him, everything I could. I called him." She stopped, put her hand to her mouth, looked at him the same way her cat had. She hadn't wanted to admit that, Greg knew. It made her seem batty, or she would worry about it making her seem that way. Marie wasn't one to let her guard down.

"Why did you call him?"

Now she was the one shrugging. "It felt like a thing I could do." She crossed her arms, pushing them up under her breasts, like they needed the hoist. "And I was angry at him. His life was exactly what a man's life should be: family, work, home. We tried to do that and we failed. GJ never even tried. Anyway, no one picked up. I hung up after seven rings. I can show you his picture if you want, though."

Marie believed in cosmic coincidences. Clairvoyance. Doppel-gangers. She wanted Idaho Greg to be GJ, had believed it for seven rings. She didn't have to say any of this to Greg for him to get it. He wanted to give her something in return.

"I went to a strip club last night." The cat darted from the room, its tail in a hook, back arched.

"Of course you did," Marie said.

"I didn't want to come here," he said. "I mean, I didn't want to keep driving." He meant driving toward anything, driving toward any kind of ending, *the journey is the destination*, he'd heard that from Marie on more than one occasion, sweet Jesus was there ever an end to his constant inward lava-hot rivers of bullshit? His middle felt as heavy as a trunk full of lead, slowly crushing his internal organs, allowing less and less oxygen into his lungs. But that's exactly how fatasses die, right?

"I think you want me to feel surprised, but I'm not surprised," she said. "You are a classic evader. That's just your way. Don't worry, now I know that it's a man's way. Most men, anyway."

Again she was saying what he'd already said, what he'd already admitted, what he'd been admitting for years, and acting like it was a newsflash. Like they were playing cat's cradle with razor wire. No wonder GJ got messed up, in the middle of all that.

"It was a waste of time," Greg said. Marie had never remarried, didn't have a partner to be alone but not lonely with, though she'd had serious boyfriends over the years, all soft-spoken, thin men who made eye contact like meeting Greg was the most important moment of their lives. All men the exact opposite of Greg. *You both want the same thing.* The sun was setting, though in Florida it could take hours to finally disappear. Rays the color of margarine were oozing through the mini-blinds, melting over the mini-jungle on the porch, making everything feel stilled, silent, already decided. Greg had finally stopped sweating. He felt the urge to say more, explain himself, fill the silence, since sitting quietly with his ex-wife, this woman who was the girl on the library steps, this woman who'd given birth to GJ, a sick man who was their son, was almost too much to bear. It felt odd, awkward, revealing, the way sex with a stranger feels. More intimate than anything else in the entire world at that very moment.

Instead he and Marie stayed quiet for a while, strangers in the waning daylight, he sunken into the couch and she perched in her chair and their son a subtle fume hovering between them, a tickle in their throats, a bruise, until the margarine changed to butter-milk and Marie finally spoke.

"I think we should get out of here," she said, leaning forward. "I'll pin your pants leg and then we should go to that area of town where he likes to hide." She meant Orange Blossom Trail, a street name that evoked the sweet scent of the flowers on an orange tree, nothing more Floridian than that, but which housed cheap motels and threadbare shacks and which most likely smelled like crack, meth, sex, death. It was home for GJ; it was where he could get what he needed, be among others like him, hide out in rooms with walls blackened by fire or mold.

"Leave my pants leg," Greg said. "I'll fit in better." He hadn't meant to be funny, had actually meant it, but Marie hooted out of her nostrils at him, and it made him laugh, too, and soon they were laughing quiet helpless laughs and wiping fat tears away. They were idiots, and they were someone's parents, and this wasn't the first time they'd laughed when laughing was the farthest thing from appropriate. They were old. GJ was aging, too. And they were about to head down OBT in Marie's grandmotherly Buick to search for him, like this was a movie starring some actors who'd also gotten old. Maybe they'd even fumble with a flashlight, or get scared when a homeless man approached and accidentally run over the man's foot as they screeched away in fear. Nothing felt real, or maybe everything felt too real. Just gestures in the dark, no one knows how to work the flashlight. Or the movie projector. Or the sun was finally gone and the sky was a black wipe of nothingness. Or too muchness. Hard to see your son in all the black, count the tiles if you can find the seams, the disco ball is missing all its mirrored tiles and yet it spins and spins. *Shut up!* Marie was holding her hands out to pull him up from the couch, something Greg considered rejecting, but the lead trunk was what it was.

Her hands were still cold, still strong and icy. Together they pulled him off the couch. "You're too big," she said. She pointed at the hard drum of his belly. "You're killing yourself." In fact, his heart was beating, thundering around his chest in a rage. From her touch? From the exertions of standing? From both? He was pathetic, just a man who stopped at a strip club on the way to see his son, a man who thrilled at the touch of a woman he hated. A woman who'd just called him fat. But he *was* fat.

"I'll keep that in mind," he said. The Band-Aid was clinging by one flesh-toned flap. He'd leave that, too. He'd go to OBT as himself, dragging along his own wounds and his own salt and sugar addictions. Everyone was just a lonely mouth, a mouth with teeth, a mouth with ventricles, a muddy hole of a mouth in the crook of someone's elbow. He wanted to ask Marie for something to eat, something to tide him over on the drive, though he wasn't hungry. Just something to do while they drove, something to focus on, something to devour. Something he could complete—ah, now he was getting somewhere! Every bite a triumph. But he'd have to wait until he was alone in the RV, alone *with* the RV, away from the wide all-seeing eyes of Marie and her cat.

"Let's start at Liquor Garage," Marie was saying. She put a small backpack on, tugged its straps until it was snug. "I can't carry a purse anymore. It hurts my back. This distributes the weight evenly." She said this last part with her palms down, like two plates of a scale; it was clearly something she'd heard the salesperson say. Marie always had some new gimmick, diet, gadget that made life make sense suddenly; then two months later she had a new thing. *Trying to be young.* Deb had carried the same purse for years, as far as Greg could remember. Again he felt thankful for Deb's simplicity. It had been only twenty-four hours since he'd seen her, a single day. How could that be possible?

"GJ got kicked out of the Garage, I thought," Greg said. It was a liquor store that had a small bar in the back, a place where you went solo and with a small stack of cash to pay for a blow job, or where you could go to watch such a thing take place. GJ had been arrested there for soliciting, though he'd told them that was a lie, he'd gone there to have a drink, not to suck someone off. He shouldn't have been doing either. GJ protested vehemently when he was lying, and he always needed money. After that Greg looked for reasons to give him what he needed. Birthdays, Christmas, even Easter, the reasons more for his own justification than for GJ's. Anything to keep him off his knees. Deb didn't approve.

"Yes, but I'm sure he's gone back since then. Or maybe someone there has seen him." They both might have said, *Well, we have to be doing* something. *Shrug.* The whole idea felt like exactly that: an idea one of them had that the other was too bored or scared or tired to say was a bad one. But it was *something.* Marie was holding the door open now, waiting for him, and Greg tried not to hobble or limp as he passed her, but it hurt to put all of his weight on his busted knee. He practiced, gingerly leaning on that leg a bit more, and then a bit more, while Marie locked up. He could see her bra line pushing into the soft flesh of her back. Again it hit him that they were old now. It was stuffy in the hallway, the only access to fresh air was the opening on each end, and where they stood the air felt canned, hot, stale. Still, Greg shuddered. *Someone's walking over your grave*, his mother used to say, her voice intrigued, suddenly excited, interested in him, now that he was dead.

A parent had called Greg at work. Greg almost didn't take the call; it had been hard, back then, to shift focus from work to home. A matrix of numbers and hidden formulas was on his screen; a printout of something nearly identical was on the desk in front of him. He had been about to highlight a row in a bright unearthly green. Green was for improvements. The sickly pink was for mistakes. "There's a woman on the line," his secretary said. "She says she's the parent of one of GJ's friends." Greg figured it was about a birthday party, or a field trip, or even a fight at school. He nearly said, *Take a message and I'll call them back*, or *Tell them to call Marie*, but he didn't. She was at one of her all-day conferences. He took the call.

"This is Greg," he said. He cradled the phone between his ear and shoulder so he could still use the highlighter.

"Did you know that your son gave my son alcohol?"

There were times throughout GJ's childhood when a moment like this occurred, and Greg recognized it as an opportunity to lose his shit or to laugh at the predictability of growing up. GJ was fourteen years old, a little young to be drinking, but it was natural for a boy to be curious and hell, he'd been sipping from Greg's beers and cocktails for a while.

"Did he, now?" He felt himself putting on the voice of a bemused parent, a father who understood, parent to parent, that kids make mistakes, a father who never lost his shit. He waited for the voice on the other end of the line to adopt the same voice, to say something like *What are we going to do with these kids?*

"My son has alcohol poisoning," the voice said. "The doctor said if he hadn't gotten his stomach pumped he could have died. They were drinking at your house."

"Is this Doyle's mother?" Doyle had been GJ's buddy lately, a short boy with big pink ears and thick ankles. A funny boy. He'd once greeted Greg with *What's crappening?*

"Of course this is Doyle's mom. Who did you think you were speaking to?" Greg had never met her, but he felt the familiar ringing in his ears that always occurred when he didn't like someone, particularly a woman someone. Particularly Marie. Maybe he should have met GJ's friends' parents. Wasn't that something parents did? Doyle once tried to give Greg the few dollars he had from his pocket, on a night when he'd offered to order the boys pizza. He seemed like a good kid. *Too good for GJ*, he found himself thinking. These kinds of thoughts were happening more and more. He found himself internally balking at the idea that he could be proud of his boy. Too egotistical. To self-celebrating. Too Marie-ish. Nobody was perfect. What he meant was, love is not unconditional. What he meant was, Doyle was not as worldly as GJ. Doyle was still an innocent.

"I'm very sorry," Greg said. He was still holding the highlighter; it was wet and slippery from his sweaty fingers. He had started sweating more and more lately, now that he'd put on a few pounds. Well, he was happy, and Deb was a good cook, and the divorce was almost final, and he would not be the one to end up alone. "What can I do? Are you at the hospital? Is GJ with you?"

"No, Mr. Reinart. This incident occurred yesterday. Doyle is already back at home. I told GJ I would wait for him to tell you, but I can see that he hasn't yet." GJ had called, Greg remembered. The night before, when he and Deb were eating dinner. He'd let it go to the answering machine. "I just thought you should know," the woman said. "They were drinking whiskey. Fourteen-year-old *boys*, Mr. Reinart."

Greg wanted, badly, to go back to the highlighting. To run the marker through the whole conversation, the whole afternoon, turning it all pink. The vertical blinds in his office window were moving gently, stirred by the air-conditioning; beyond that, the highway and the highway crossing it and the highway underneath that unfurled and invaded and grew like cement ivy, cars fleeing in either direction, the sun running its glinting diamonds across their hoods.

Yesterday had been a Monday. He'd dropped GJ off at school after his weekend with him. So GJ must have waited for his car to drive off, and then he and Doyle must have gone right back to the house to drink. Why his house, though? Why not Marie's condo? He felt his face get warm. GJ was trying to make a statement. A *fuck you, Dad* kind of statement. *If you don't watch it, children will walk all over you.* Greg's mother, standing in the kitchen, talking to a weeping neighbor. *You can't let them get the upper hand.* At the time, Greg had thought, *Oh, bullshit.* He didn't walk all over his mother, because she was impervious. He could do something to make her proud or he could shit on her prized linoleum and her reaction would have been the same: eyes on him like they were trying to bring him into focus, like he was someone she recognized but couldn't quite place, then a slow, accusing drag of her cigarette, and then he would break eye contact and it would be over. Her neighborly advice was bullshit, did not jibe with who she was as a mother, but now Greg felt his heart beat faster, that acidy flip in his stomach; was GJ trying to make a fool of him?

He had once gone too far, himself. There had been more than one incident, actually, but only one time when GJ saw it happen, when he was around eleven years old. They'd gone to Mick's, had ordered burgers and fries and onion rings, one of Mick's thin milk-shakes for GJ and beer after beer for Greg. At some point he must have switched to whiskeys, neat, just that gorgeous caramelly slosh two fingers up the scratched glass, that warm bite in his throat. Then suddenly he'd been outside, flat on his back in the parking lot, looking up at a man who he first thought was trying to help him up before realizing it had been the man who'd put him down. His own blood was running into his mouth; his nose felt like a shattered coffee mug. The man who hit him had his hands on GJ's shoulders, was bent over talking into the boy's face, though GJ's eyes were on Greg, watching him try to stand, try not to throw up, then throwing up as discreetly as he could, in between his dress shoes, each heave making his nose feel reshattered. It was Mick himself, the man who had hit him. Greg had celebrated birth-days, promotions, his divorce, all at Mick's. He'd taken GJ there that night to celebrate the boy's good report card. And now Greg had to watch, thick mucus on his chin, as Mick held his son by the shoulders to the earth. Had to allow his boy to lead him to a cab, to dab at his slacks with the white rag Mick had shoved at Greg for his nose. *What did he tell you?* Greg asked GJ, over and over. *What did he say about me?* Finally, GJ answered. *He said sometimes people need their asses kicked. He said you'd been needing it a long time.* The cabbie watched them in the rearview. *Don't stain my leather*, he kept saying. *Fifty bucks extra if you stain my leather.* Greg held his head back, wiped the slowing blood into his own mouth so he wouldn't stain the leather. He was suddenly sober, each beat of his heart a firework of pain in his nose. GJ watched out the window. When they got home, Greg gave GJ all the cash he had, a couple hundred dollars. He had wanted to give the boy something, for his report card, as an apology, as a way of thanking him for not crying, for not losing his shit. The next day they told Marie that Greg had been hit by a ball at the batting cages. He had wanted to ask GJ what he'd done, why he needed his ass kicked, but he couldn't risk bringing it up again, not when it seemed as hazy as a dream, a nightmare, something they both woke up from and felt relieved was over.

"Thank you for letting me know," Greg said. "I'm sorry about Doyle."

"Your son is different than he used to be," Doyle's mother said. "He's not the same."

"Yes, I know what the word *different* means," Greg said. He suddenly felt hot with anger at this woman, this woman who presumed to know anything about his son, who would not accept his apology.

"I'm glad that you do," the woman said. "You know, Doyle's father and I divorced when he was a baby, so he never had to be a part of . . . all that. It can be hard on a child." She hung up the phone, so gently that Greg thought she was just taking a pause, until the dial tone kicked in, hollering loud and dull.

It was almost two-thirty; GJ would be getting out of school soon, getting on the bus, walking the three blocks to Marie's condo. Greg capped both highlighters and put on his suit coat, which was getting tight in the shoulders. He took it off and slung it over his arm. He dinged his elbow on the doorjamb on his way out, his secretary yelling out a surprised "Oh!"

"I'm fine," he said. And then in the elevator on the way down he said it again to his reflection in the gold mirrored walls: "I'm fine." Since he was a boy, it had felt good to say things out loud to himself. It made everything more real; it made him feel like he was transcending the shape-shifting unreality of the world by attempting to define it. *Today is Tuesday. I work on the fourteenth floor, which is actually the thirteenth floor, but the superstitious idiots who designed the building refused to name it that. My son . . .* He wasn't sure how to complete the sentence. *My son needs his ass kicked—there, that did the trick.*

GJ was nearly home when Greg drove up, walking slowly along the curb since there was no sidewalk leading in to the condo, just marshy, wet grass. His face when he bent into the open window of Greg's car was an alarming shade of red, his hair stuck to his forehead in wet points and the sweet smell of hot sweat coming off the boy in waves, like steam from a pot.

"Get in," Greg said.

"It's okay, I can walk."

"You know why I'm here?"

"Of course." GJ often came off like he knew the answer before anyone, had made his peace with it hours ago. He got that from his mother. Intuition sharp as a blade. It felt like mind reading sometimes. But sometimes he gave them both too much credit. Of course GJ knew why he was here; it had happened only the day before.

"Get in," Greg said again. *You have a scary mouth sometimes,* Marie had told him once. *It gets small and white.* He felt his mouth doing that now. He had been terrified of his mother, had never talked back to her or crossed her in any way because of it. He hadn't done a good enough job of making his son afraid of him. He'd wanted the boy to know him in a way he'd never known his mother. He waited for GJ to buckle up, and then he slapped the boy, the angle of his body and the closeness in the car making it more of a cuff on the ear.

GJ put his hand up to his cheek. Already his hands were larger than Greg's. The boy was going to be enormous, a tall, slouching creature with Greg's face. And then GJ laughed. A quiet snuffling from his nostrils that Greg first took for crying, but no, the boy was laughing, trying to hold it in with both his hands now. Greg coasted and then parked along the road outside the condo gates. He did not know what else to do. He and Marie had made a promise never to hit their child; they'd both been whipped and hit and tossed as children. But they had both gone back on that promise with GJ.

"I don't understand why you're laughing," Greg said. "Your friend could have died."

"It's just funny to me," GJ said. "Not Doyle. That's not funny. You're funny. This is exactly how I pictured you reacting, and now we're here."

Doyle's mother was right; GJ wasn't the same. He was talking to Greg like he knew him in a different way. He had taken the money from Greg that night after what happened at Mick's. He had taken it as easily as if it was money he was owed from a job he did.

"You could have gone to jail," Greg said.

"Doyle's mother said she didn't want to press charges."

"You could have died." Greg realized he didn't know enough about what had happened; he didn't know anything, really. What time had they started drinking? What was GJ wearing? When did he know Doyle wasn't okay? Why didn't anyone call him—the cops, the hospital, anyone? Did Marie know?

"I didn't drink any of it," GJ said.

"What?"

"Yeah, I didn't want any. Doyle wanted to try it and he drank it like it was a Pepsi or something. I just watched him."

Greg looked at his son, who would not look at him aside from quick darting glances. The glances of someone who had something to hide. Or who had something to protect. His black hair was getting long; there were some curls in the back now, something girls probably liked. He had his backpack in his lap, crumpled in a way that made Greg realize there probably weren't any books in there, no way for him to do his homework. His T-shirt had a hole at the shoulder revealing painfully white skin underneath, the same pale skin he had as a baby. He had Marie's coloring but Greg's features. It was hard to look at the boy and not see Marie, though Deb told him the boy looked more like him than her.

"Why didn't you want any?" Greg asked.

"Oh, you know . . ." GJ looked out his window, plucked something off the side mirror, brought it into the car. Greg saw that it was a ladybug, a delicate red bead that GJ was letting crawl across his hand. "I just didn't want to." He shook his hand out the window and the ladybug flew away. He pushed open the door and got out. He leaned back in through the window.

"Next time I'll try harder," he said, and laughed again, that laugh his whole face tried to hide, his lips tightening and his eyes bulging and the laugh escaping only in quick bursts of air from his nostrils.

Greg watched him walk through the side gate, unlocking it with a key around his neck. He'd left a warm moisture behind him that filled Greg's car. He had no idea who that boy was, that stranger with jeans that were too short, that young man with the rolled, defeated shoulders walking slowly away from Greg, no rush, nothing to run from or fear. That stranger who was his son.

S o why did you stop at a strip club, really?" Marie asked. She had one hand on the wheel and the other on the bulb of the gearshift, as if it were a manual transmission like she had in their early days together, that shitty, shit-brown Dodge. "I mean, in general. What's in it for the men who go to those places?"

"It varies, I guess," Greg said. An answer that wasn't an answer, his specialty when they were married. He fit comfortably in the passenger seat of Marie's Buick, a small miracle. There was enough room for his legs, enough room for his gut. He said a silent thank-you to the Buick gods, or he said it to Marie, or he said it to nobody and nothing. The sky was a purply gray now, the skin of a car-crash victim. Greg had forgotten how Marie liked to push hard on the brakes, then push hard on the gas when she wanted to get going. He'd also forgotten how hot the insides of cars were, before the AC kicked in; he'd forgotten how Marie always had a paper strawberry hanging from the rearview mirror, swinging idly, ejecting plumes of canned scent that was supposed to refresh but instead coated his tongue in what tasted like old Juicy Fruit and hairspray. His mouth watered the way it did when he needed to vomit. Marie rolled his window down using her driver-side controls; she always knew. She always knew everything, except for the stuff that mattered. Like how the tone of her voice—that . . . *haughtiness* was how Greg had come to view it—made his spine shudder inside his body. How his body physically rejected the sound. She didn't know that. And she didn't know how to cure GJ. And she didn't know where to find him. But she knew when Greg was about to be sick, congratulations to her. The air coming in through the car was hot, too, but it helped, and Greg opened his mouth so it could fish out the taste of the air freshener. Marie's car was tidy, too tidy, like those model homes they'd looked at back when they were buying a house. Everything in its place, not even a pen sticking out of the cup holder. Why did she think she needed that strawberry shit?

"You're real Florida, now," he said.

Marie switched on her blinker; they were about to get back onto the highway he'd gotten off an hour before. "Am I, now?"

Greg pointed at the strawberry. "Only Floridians use these dumb things."

"That's not true," Marie said. She seemed like she was about to say something else, her mouth open and inhaling, but she decided against it. She eased the Buick onto the highway, the blinker still tock-tock-tocking, all the way until she had merged. She reached over and pulled the air freshener off the mirror, tossed it in Greg's lap. "Put it in the glove compartment."

There was nothing in there, either, aside from a small packet of tissues. Greg tossed the strawberry in. Now that his stomach had calmed he felt better, able, unafraid, despite knowing that they were pointing the Buick directly toward squalor, toward trash and fire, toward sex and crime and death. The Buick felt solid as a tank; maybe that was it.

"I mean it, though," Marie said. "You went to those kinds of places when we were married, and you go to them now. So you weren't going because of me. You were going for some other reason, right? What draws you to a strip club? What calls to you?" *Calls to you.* Marie believed in callings.

"Why are you so interested?" It was hard not to feel interrogated; she asked and asked until there was an answer that made sense to her, even if it didn't make sense to Greg.

"You know how it is these days," she said. She was going exactly the speed limit, strolling along in the right lane, and cars were passing her in angry blurs. "You think a lot about the past. You wonder about stuff. You have questions."

"These days?"

She laughed, that same husk of a laugh she always used when she felt like doing the opposite of laughing. "We're old, G." She hadn't called him that in years. "I'll be fifty-nine this year. In my head I've been forty-two all this time. Sometimes twelve. What age do you think you are?"

Forty-one. That was the age he always thought he was. The year he met Deb, when the world felt split open and the light was oozing in. Like he had been a cantaloupe seed all that time and the divorce was that blessed heavy mallet that smithereened it all, that freed him. "I'll be fifty-nine, too," he said.

"I look at myself in the mirror, like I'm doing right now." She adjusted the rearview so she could see her own face. "Who is that old lady? When GJ was born I was young. He had a young mother, and now his mother is old. I could be the grandmother to his children, if he had any."

She had slowed down, totally focused on her own face now. A car behind them swerved around the Buick. Greg reached over and readjusted the rearview, positioning it away from her face. "GJ is older than we were when we had him," he said. He didn't know what he meant, saying that to her. He'd been thinking about it on the drive; he hadn't stopped thinking about it.

"I know what you're saying," Marie said. She had both hands on the wheel now. Greg knew she was gathering herself back up, all the shards she'd just spilled. "We were adults when we were his age, but he's still a child."

"Yes, exactly," Greg said. *He's still a child.* Why did that feel like such a relief?

"I don't think I ever truly let him be a kid. Do you?" She faced him, the car drifting to the right.

"Eyes on the road," he said gently, grateful he didn't have to answer. She was right, though. He could think of a hundred times, five hundred times maybe, when GJ bore witness to something he shouldn't have had to. "Cocktail hour," for one, something he and Marie devised in GJ's toddlerhood, something to make the evenings still feel special, festive, doable. Both of them got more and more sloppy as the evening wore on, sometimes with neighbors or friends or coworkers, but mostly just the three of them. GJ's little face, watching them, that questioning smile, *Are we happy? Is this funny? Am I in on the joke?* He wanted so badly to be a part of it. Marie wasn't a drinker until they both were. She could take it or leave it. How lucky for her. Maybe it was her way of fighting for the marriage by plunging into whatever hole Greg was in. But they took GJ with them. Crying, yelling, laughing, snoring, staring, GJ saw it all. Why didn't they just get on the floor and play trucks with him? Tickle him, draw with him, anything. Would it have been so hard, so impossible?

It would have been impossible. Even now Greg felt antsy, the pull of the liquor cabinet, the beers under the dinette in the RV, the Arby's and the Popeye's and the Pizza Huts whizzing by, so many missed chances.

He remembered one night when GJ was older, in second or third grade, and Marie had reached over and cheersed his new gut. *Here's to you, Santy Claus!* she said, and they both laughed at him. Ha ha, Dad is as fat as Santa! It was something his mother would have said, elbowing one of her girlfriends and telling him to twirl. He knocked the drink out of Marie's hand before he could stop himself, the vodka and lemon splashing into GJ's hair. He was too angry to be thankful for it at the time, but GJ just kept laughing. He was delighted, in fact. Thought they were all just being silly. The mercy in that child's heart, Greg knew he'd never deserved it. Would never deserve it. But if GJ was still a child, there might be mercy still.

Marie pulled the car over, jerking it to a stop on the shoulder. Mists of dust plumed up around the Buick, like it was part of a disappearing magic trick. "It makes me angry," she said. "It makes me really *fucking* angry." Greg always hated when Marie said the f-word. Every letter pronounced, drenched in hatred, like a wet dress she'd pulled from a stranger's suitcase and forced herself to try on. The Buick had felt as spacious as a loft, room for their bodies and small talk, but there was not enough room for this.

"Do you want me to drive?" he asked. Then he remembered that Marie said no to all questions when she was upset, like a toddler. "I'll drive." He reached around his gut to unbuckle his seat belt, but she put her hand over his to stop him, her fake nails grazing his skin, dulled and harmless and sad as a clipped beak.

"Why aren't you angry?" She looked at him, that studious look on her face; it truly was bizarre, how little people changed. He had shut a door when they'd divorced; he'd shut another door when he and Deb settled in West Virginia. A whole hallway of doors, shut tight. And yet here he was, all of them flung wide open, spilling light or dark and noise or silence, all leading right back to Marie, this woman he'd tried to escape for years. *Family is family* (shut up, Mother!). He *was* angry, only not the way Marie demanded. He was angry at time, how it bent and careened and led you right back to the beginning, how it made strangers of loved ones, how it made family of strangers. He was angry at his big body. If he was felled at the waist there'd be rings of fat showing that he was a million years old, not forty-one, not fifty-nine. He had to carry the years of blubber around; Marie had her fake nails and lonely condo; GJ had oblivion.

"We don't know where he is, Marie."

"I know that," she said. She took her hand back. "Why doesn't that make you angry? Half of our lives, we've been worried about him. Half of our lives! I want it all back." She was miming pulling a rope in, hand over hand, like the rope was unspooling from where Greg sat. "Give it all back to me."

"You'll never get it back," Greg said. He shocked himself with the kind tone in his voice. This was at least something he knew, something he'd known for years, at least all those years in West Virginia staring out the plate-glass window at the treetops and wheeling birds and colorless sky and his own widening reflection. The grandfather clock whispering the passing seconds, growing desperate and shouting out the hour. Hour after hour, day after day. Twenty-four hours in a day. Sixty minutes in an hour. Sixty seconds in a minute. All divisible by three, which is one and one and one. This was it; the only turning back was in his head now. Remembering. Examining. And then discarding. *Today is Tuesday, that much I know.* "It's gone."

A police car pulled up next to the Buick, and the cop in the passenger seat gestured for Marie to roll the window down. "We're fine, Officer," Marie called. "Just needed a breather. But thank you." The officer, a woman with hair the color and texture of those curly noodles in soup cups, leaned over so she could see past Marie to get a look at Greg. He held his hand up in a wave, then a salute. Nothing to see here, just a pair of old goofs.

"Move along," the officer said, her voice as hard and dense as a stone.

"Sure thing," Marie said. When the cop car pulled away she turned to Greg and said, "Well, then, don't you want the rest of your life?" As if the conversation had never been interrupted. "If we can't get those years back, then I want the remaining years I have to be mine. Finally mine."

Marie had lived alone for at least a decade, GJ coming and going, but mostly going, living with girlfriends or drug friends or, in the brief pockets of sobriety, living in his own room in a half-way house downtown. In Greg's mind those years had been hers and hers alone. But maybe he wasn't the only one in a holding pattern. Maybe Marie had stared the paint off her walls, too, waiting for release.

Marie put on the blinker, craned her neck over her left shoulder to watch for an opportunity. "When my mother was sixty," she said, pulling the car onto the highway, "she had white hair and wore her glasses on a chain and embroidered pillows and drank prune juice out of a Dixie cup every morning. She was a granny."

"You're not a granny," Greg said.

"She wouldn't be caught dead going where we're going, anyway," she said. It was clear this was the story Marie told herself. If she had not yet turned into her mother, if she had not yet given in to age, then there was still time. If GJ was still a child, then there was still time; that was Greg's story. Time for what, though? All Greg had was time and it didn't make a difference.

"This is it," Marie said. A bright green sign said ORANGE BLOSSOM TRAIL, NEXT RIGHT. The sun had made a flamingo-pink line of the horizon, its final gaudy act before disappearing for the night. Now he felt a bit afraid, a black seed sprouting in his stomach. He found himself wondering if Marie actually did have a flashlight, though there wasn't one to be seen in the neat confines of the Buick. Not even a crowbar or an ice scraper, since it was Florida, after all; neither of them had a weapon. He truly was old. The few times he'd driven down OBT he hadn't been bothered. The few people he did see walked along the sidewalks like they were sleepwalking, hiding from the sun beating down, or the drugs flooding their veins, or simply trying to pass for normal so they wouldn't be stopped or ogled at. Who did he think he would be swinging a crowbar at? West Virginia had its OBT, he knew, probably in the mountains if TV was to be believed, but he'd never had to visit.

There were palm trees here, too, waving their fronds over broken sidewalks and in the parking lots of strip clubs and boarded-up motels and bars. Chain link stretched everywhere, like OBT was an abandoned prison. People collected on corners and outside gas-station shops, talking and gesturing, like flies in glue traps. Black, white, Hispanic, a true melting pot of misery. In the final moments of daylight Greg could see a woman in a short dress walking along the sidewalk, slowly, like she was tiptoeing, and when they passed her Greg saw that she'd broken a heel and was in fact up on her toes. Marie turned on her brights; most of the streetlamps were out and the dark was coming fast.

"It's just up here," she said. The primary colors of the Liquor Garage sign loomed ahead, the green G burned out. As they got closer they could see another clump of people outside the door, waiting or watching or doing nothing, it was hard to tell. "I have some mace in my purse," she said. If he'd been at home watching this on the television, he'd have hoped these two old fools wouldn't be so clichéd, would have some compassion, see these clumps as human beings, each with his or her own story, each with a mother and father or children of their own. But as Marie's headlights washed over the gathering, as they shifted and cringed in the brightness, Greg felt afraid, terrified even, of what might happen. This was where GJ spent time; these were his people. Greg loved a good bar. Wood tables, sticky floors, the smell of grease and beer, waitresses looking just past his face as they waited on his order. The warm coziness, a place to let the sounds of televisions and small talk and the thick silence between songs cradle him like a hammock. He had taken it too far once or twice. But the Garage was something different. It was the end stop. It was where people came when there was nowhere else to go. And so Greg didn't want to see any of them as anything. He just wanted to crane his neck and spot his son among them, pull him into the Buick and drive on. But GJ was not in this clump, Greg could see. They'd have to get out of the car and go inside. Marie parked the car as close to the door as the crowd would allow.

"Okay," she said. "Let's get this over with."

A man with dirt clouding his face broke free from the crowd

and walked over to the Buick. Marie rolled down her window and the black seed in Greg's belly burst. She was not her mother, frail and pruned. She was no granny. She would face this head-on.

"Hello," she said.

The man had crouched down so he could peer into the car. Up close he looked young, younger than GJ, maybe. His hair was stiff and foul; he was smiling and Greg was relieved to see that his teeth were still mostly white. "You looking for a date?" he asked. His voice was high and feminine.

"We're looking for our son. His name is GJ. Sometimes he goes by Greg?" Marie was leaning far back into her seat, probably trying to escape the man's stench.

The man looked at Greg. His eyes weren't right; they looked like they'd been put in a cup and shaken. "Don't know him," he said. Now his voice was deeper. "But y'all need to be careful out here." He said it like a warning, an unwelcoming. He stood and turned to the clump. "We got slummers," he shouted. "Look out, look out, they might getcha."

Was the man talking about them? Were they the dangerous ones in this crowd? Or was it another warning for Greg and Marie? The man pushed between two others, who wandered off in different directions as if being separated had unleashed them, freed them. One sat on the hood of Marie's car, his back to them; the other walked through the parking lot and out onto the sidewalk before the darkness closed ranks and he disappeared.

The man on the hood wore a shirt that said *Christ Is King*, a crude stick-figure Jesus on a cross forming the *t* in *Christ*. Marie honked the horn, two quick blasts. The man slid off and looked back over his shoulder at them like he'd been insulted.

"I did call the cops," Marie said. She rolled her window back up and turned off the ignition.

"When?" Greg asked. He hadn't seen her dialing; he hadn't seen her phone at all.

"The first week GJ was gone. They said since he's an adult with a history of drug use there's not much they can do."

"Oh," Greg said. Sometimes he felt grateful such a word existed, a small breath of a word, a pebble, really, but one that didn't tether him to anything. *Oh.* He hadn't called the cops. Again he faced that thing, that something that felt like it was on the tip of his tongue. What was it? He believed GJ could be found. But there was something else, something attached to that. The man from the hood of the car stood and wandered into the bar, the Buick rocking gently as it released his weight.

"I said thank you and hung up," Marie said. She was threading her house keys and car key in between each knuckle, so they stood out like spikes. "I just let it go and then two weeks went by like a snap."

"I know what you mean," Greg said. He was thinking of his own long afternoons, how they passed by in arcs he could trace: the sunlight in this corner, the sun apexing, the sunlight in the other corner now. The ticker-tape endlessness of the news channel. Mute, unmute. The living room holding him in place, a model home representation of a life, all he had to do was blend in. He hadn't felt allowed to leave. He hadn't felt allowed to panic, or cry, or start some kind of online campaign, or print flyers or even a T-shirt. All of that felt like something he saw on TV; all of it felt senseless and exhausting and—

"After this," Marie was saying, "I really don't know what else we can do. What I can do. If we don't find him tonight." She was looking at him, really looking at him, that classic Marie deep eye contact that had always unnerved Greg but that felt particularly unfair now, in the closeness of the Buick, with a crowd of strangers

looking on, outside what felt like the entry to hell on earth. It hit
Greg that she was asking for permission.

"You've done enough," he said. He wanted to pat her hand but
she was still holding the keys. She had done enough. GJ had lived
with her, not Greg, all these years, all those offs and ons. It was
her wallet that went light, her guest bedroom that grew dingy
with GJ's filth, her eyes that saw him on good days and bad. She
took him to job interviews at the mall; she picked him up at the bus
stop when he was inevitably fired. Under Marie's watch the boy
had passed his GED test, gotten his diploma. Greg had long suspected she'd somehow taken the GED for GJ, but it had been a
relief for Greg, this arrangement. A boy should be with his mother
was what he told himself. But he also just didn't have it in him.
Somehow, Marie did. Or had. Now she was tapping out.

A boy should be with his mother. A freeing thing and a damning
one. Greg on his daily circuit of nothing, doing nothing, being
nothing. Now at least one of those things wasn't true anymore.

"We'll ask around inside and then we'll go home," Greg said.

Marie nodded; it had been what she wanted to hear. She used
her free hand to sling her backpack purse over her shoulder and
then across her body, wearing it on her front instead of her back.
"He might not want us to find him, you know," she said. "Some
people do that."

"That's true," Greg said. He'd seen a handful of true-crime
TV shows where an adult went missing only to be found decades
later, living a totally new life. They'd left behind shitty spouses,
sad family lives, loneliness. Greg wasn't sure if GJ was sober enough
to feel lonely, or to devise a plan to begin anew. When was the last
time GJ seemed like himself? Greg tried to remember. It had been
a long time. Addicts and teenagers hide themselves from their
families, and GJ had been both. There had been one Christmas—

GJ was about sixteen or seventeen—when Greg gave him a computer. Deb's idea. *Maybe it'll get him excited about school again*, she'd said. And GJ had seemed genuinely surprised, happy. Like he knew what an extravagance it was. They ate pizza by the electric fireplace that night, a family tradition, admiring the twinkle lights on the Christmas tree and watching funny movies. The next morning, when Marie came to the door to fetch him, GJ had shown her the computer with what seemed like great pride. *That must have been expensive*, Marie had said. Back then she could have been the president of a fan club dedicated to his finances; she kept track of every detail. But that Christmas was the last time GJ had seemed like himself. Or had seemed like the possibility of a self. Later Greg found out that GJ pawned the computer.

"Take my mace," Marie said. She held out a small black canister to him.

"No thanks." Holding her mace, the crude key spikes, her purse across her body, Marie looked as afraid as he felt. And as old. He wanted his hands to be empty when they walked in, ready for anything. When GJ was an infant they used to look at each other, sleepless and stunned, and say, *Can you believe we made this?* It was a way to remind themselves that there had been a time before, that they had brought this being into being. He wanted that again, that astonishment. *Can you believe we made this? We.* That he'd had that with Marie, this old woman next to him, was a different kind of astonishing, a sadder one. He opened his door and got out, and Marie did the same.

"They'll getcha!" the man yelled again, pointing at them over the crowd. Greg put his hand up in a wave. It seemed like the only thing to do. The air felt stalled, the same oxygen passed from mouth to mouth, exhaled in a hot mist that clung to Greg's clothing. He held the door for Marie.

The liquor store part of the Garage was about five rows of spirits, with a back wall of refrigerators and double doors leading into the bar area. The heat carried on inside, though it seemed to be coming from somewhere in the ceiling. He had heard of places blasting icy air-conditioning to keep people from lingering. Maybe the Garage was attempting something similar.

"Wine coolers are two for one. Beers are not sold separately. You break, you buy," the cashier called out. He was a small man with a neat ponytail sitting behind thick Plexiglas, leaning on his elbows over a magazine, and Greg could not tell if he'd even looked up at them.

"We're not here to buy anything," Marie said. She walked over to the Plexiglas and rapped on it with her keys. "Hi," she said when the man looked up. "We're looking for our son, a man named GJ. Or maybe you know him as Greg?"

"GJ, huh?" The man had a thin, wet mouth. He ran his thumb and forefinger down its outer corners. His forehead was oily, a wet ring circling his shirt collar.

"Yes," Marie said. She was cradling her purse the way she used to cradle her pregnant belly. He hadn't thought of that in years. He could suddenly see her standing in their tiny kitchen, laughing. *He's kicking a lot!* She'd known it was a boy; Marie always knew. "He's been missing for three weeks now."

"Yeah, I think I know who you mean," the man said. "Geej. Tall guy, right?"

"Yes!" Marie turned to Greg; her face was hopeful, excited. Could it really be this easy?

"I haven't seen him around in a while," the man said. He looked down, back to his magazine, which Greg could now see was a *Penthouse*. A woman knelt on a wooden chair, displaying thin buttocks.

"Oh," Marie said.

"When was the last time you saw him?" Greg asked.

"I don't know, man." The cashier licked his fingertip and turned the page. Now the woman was sitting in the chair, her legs spread.

Marie went to the closest aisle and grabbed a bottle. She placed it inside the Plexiglas box in front of the cashier, who would have to take it out on the other side to scan it. "We'll take this," she said. "And then maybe you'll remember something." A bribe! Greg was flooded with gratitude. A bribe, of course!

The man squinted at the box. "Triple sec, huh? It's forty," he said, without even removing it.

Marie pushed two twenties through the thin pay slot. The man placed them in the fold of his magazine, one on top of the other, and closed it gently. He looked up at them, running his fingers down the corners of his mouth again. He was such a small man, Greg thought. Dainty. A bird. The opposite of GJ.

"I haven't seen him in a while," the cashier said. "The last time I saw him was maybe a couple weeks ago. He came in and went to the back like always. Me and the owner know he steals from us. He owes us." He nodded at the closed magazine. "That doesn't even begin to cover it." He looked at them sternly, like they had been the ones to steal. The door opened and a couple walked in, keeping their heads down, holding each other and shuffling to the bar in the back.

"But we let him still come in because he's a nice person deep down. He has a good heart."

"Yes," Marie said. She moved closer to the cashier, pressing her purse into the counter. "That's exactly right."

"He pays when he can, unlike some of the other ones."

The other ones. In the cashier's mind, GJ was just one of the clump. In Greg's mind, a man who stole but paid when he could was still a thief.

"He usually comes in at least once a week, but like I said, it's been a little while since I've seen him. Sometimes people just move on." The door opened again and a man in a red baseball hat walked in; Greg could smell the sharp odor of what he'd been drinking.

"Beers are *not* sold separately," the cashier called after the man. He shook his head and looked back at Greg. "If you wouldn't mind, put that bottle back where you found it on your way out."

Marie took the bottle out of the case and put it back on the shelf, and then walked toward the back where the bar was. Greg followed. Just before they pushed through the double doors, he saw the man in the red hat wrestle a beer from a six-pack and drop it down the front of his pants.

The bar was a square room with moldy tiles for flooring. They gave under Greg's feet as he walked in. He'd so easily forgotten how everything in Florida *gave*; every surface marshy, damp, loamy. The only sources of light were a purple lava lamp at the far end of the room that was fighting a slow clog and a thin railing of fluorescence running just under the bar's edge. The other patrons appeared hewn from shadow, if shadow had the texture of ash: just visible enough. The couple that had just walked in were sitting in bean bags, the woman's legs splayed and her feet pointing in like a puppet whose strings had just been cut. Her skirt had ridden up and the flesh from her thighs seemed to spill out, like she was a fluid and not a solid. "Oh, don't worry about her, man," her companion yelled. Greg had been staring. "She's just tired."

The bar ran three sides of a square. The farthest side was where you went if you wanted something more than a drink. Greg had been here before, once, years and years ago when it got bad with Marie. A woman with curly red hair helped him out that day, on the far side of the bar, in the darkness that felt like another room.

No lava lamp back then, but it had been daytime, possibly even a workday. The woman had thick glasses that made her eyes look like fish caught in a bowl. He'd kept his elbows on the bar, had tapped for another drink during. What had he felt that day? He remembered the feel of the woman's molars, the tired feeling in his legs and crotch, the way the brightness of the day hurt his eyes when he left out the back . . . He had felt triumph. A calming sense of liberation. He was peeling himself from Marie, strip by strip. It was why he didn't want the mace, or the keys, or the cops, coming in here: over the years those strips had wilted, liquefied, congealed into shame. Nothing worked right; he flopped and jiggled inside and out. He had done some things; who hadn't? And he had done them willingly. He wanted away from the life he'd created with Marie. At its core there was nothing to be ashamed of there. But he hadn't known how to do it. There was no road map, no itemized checklist, no formula. A coworker once went a week sleeping on the love seat in his office, shaving in the hallway bathroom. Smiling always, smiling like an idiot, cheersing his coffee mug at Greg in the mornings, everyone pretending like the man wasn't drenched in pathetic. That kind of gesture wasn't for Greg. Instead he had done something that day, that bright bright day in the bar he was standing in now, which smelled exactly as he remembered it: cigarettes and mixed drinks and armpits gone sour. He'd driven home feeling triumphant after allowing a stranger to put her mouth on him in a bar. It had been his winnings, and now it was his legacy.

Marie was crouched by the bean bags, her hand on the sprawled woman's knee, leaning in to the man's face. Asking him about GJ. Greg walked over. "I'm going to show him a picture," Marie said. The man grinned up at Greg. She dug in her purse for her phone, held it up so the man could see a picture showing GJ with his arm around Marie, her head resting on his chest, both of them laughing. It was from one of the times that GJ had been well, those brief weeks or months when his eyes were clear and he smiled easily and, according to Marie, he slept nearly around the clock.

"Naw," the man said. He shook his head at the phone. For a moment Greg felt defensive, as if this man were rejecting his son, just another useless emotion he didn't need. "Don't know him."

There were a few others scattered around the place, two men leaning over the bar, a woman leaning against the far corner, the bartender sitting hunched on a stool wearing a faded and torn Liquor Garage T-shirt, its letters glowing out from his chest.

"Let's go," Greg shouted to Marie. She stood, brushed off her knees.

"Don't you want to talk to those people over there?"

"No. He's not here. This is a waste of time." He felt desperate to leave, desperate to quit pretending at this game of P.I. that he and Marie were losing. GJ hadn't looked like the man in that photo in quite some time. Greg could be back at the condo, back in the RV loft, in half an hour. He walked back through the double doors, down the aisle of mixers, away from the colorful glass in the refrigerated cases, such a cheerful sight to him usually.

"Safe drive," the cashier called. Greg held the door for Marie, the heat pulling at their clothes, swallowing them whole.

"Hey." A scrawny boy had broken off from the clump. His nose bloomed with acne, pearls of tapioca balanced one atop another. "I heard you was looking for your son."

Marie pulled out her phone again, held it up for the boy to see.

"Yeah, I see, I see," he said. "I think they got him." He jerked his head, looking just beyond Greg's shoulder. "They get him sometimes."

"Who?" Marie asked. "Who gets him?"

"Them," the boy said. He widened his eyes; he became a mask. He looked at Greg. "They," he whispered. And then, louder: "They."

The clump burst into laughter, breaking apart to thump one another's backs, rejoining like an octopus drawing in its tentacles. The boy with the ruined nose backed away from Greg and Marie, laughing now, holding his pants up with one hand and covering his mouth with the other.

"Go home, white folks," one of the clump yelled, and there was laughter again, the white people in the clump, it appeared to Greg, laughing the hardest.

Y-ball. T-ball. Pop Warner. Tap dance (Marie's idea). Soccer. Cub Scouts. Baseball. Football. Piano lessons (Marie's idea). Guitar lessons. Boy Scouts. Almost to Eagle; kicked out. Journals, sketch pads, canvases. Crayons, markers, paints. Charcoal. Spray paint. Skateboard. Body board. Beach summers. Sky-blue swimming pools. Hotels. Resorts. Camping. Hamburgers, pizza, hot dogs, ice cream. Falafel, grape leaves, hummus. Enchiladas. Casseroles. Nachos. Candy. Soda. Slurpees. Big Gulps. Beer. Whiskey. Dope. Hash. Tar. Rocks. Spoon, needle. Pipe. Darkness. Light. I'm sorry. It's okay. Theft. Shouting. Crying. Darkness. Light. I'm sorry. It's okay. Dope, dope, dope, rope-a-dope. Darkness. Nothing, no goodbye, gone, absent. No smell no color no noise. I'm sorry. It's okay.

Greg was having a dream that he and GJ were in a coffin, *It's a double wide, Dad, room for both of us,* and they laughed, took turns knocking on the lid, polite raps, no rush, no terror about being buried alive, just patient knocks, three-two-one. He woke but the knocking continued; it was Marie, knocking on the door of the RV. He rolled into a crouch and pushed off with his fists, landing on the floor on his bare flat feet.

She was holding a plate with a bagel on it, a pretty white skirt of cream cheese around the edges that made Greg's mouth water. One wouldn't be enough, but it would have to be.

"So you're leaving today?" she asked, sitting on the small bench across from the dinette. She was wearing what looked like the exact same pants and blouse as the day before; everyone had a uniform, Greg was realizing. Or at least everyone their age did.

"I am," he said. He bit into the bagel, still warm, crunchy on the outside and tender on the inside, perfect.

"Last night was a bust."

He nodded, took another bite. This would be a four-bite bagel. He didn't want to think about the night before, how they'd driven home in silence, how Greg had walked to his RV without saying good night, both of them defeated and silly and useless and *relieved*.

"Where are you going next?"

He swallowed too soon, the bagel rough and barnacled as it slid down his throat. He had considered, before drifting off to sleep the night before, driving all day back to West Virginia, calling Deb from the parking lot of the RV rental place, eating a spaghetti dinner, and sleeping in his own bed. Weighing his options from there. Filing a missing person's report, or starting a Facebook page, calling the local news. The idea that he would find GJ by lumbering around in the RV was feeling less noble now, and more foolish. The fate of the aging man: every action, if looked at from a certain angle, was a joke. "I might go home," he said. "Unless you have a better idea."

She leaned back, crossed her arms under her breasts. "Maybe you could go to your father's."

The bagel felt lodged just beyond his heart, holding steady there like a rock plugging a geyser. "You think GJ is at my dad's?" He hadn't considered that possibility, not for a second. His father lived in a ground-floor apartment in the tower of an assisted-living community about a three-hour drive from Marie's. Senility had given him bursts of meanness; he'd already been given "a warning," for pushing an aide when she'd tried to take his temperature. He did not like to talk on the phone, did not like visitors, and Deb's yearly Christmas gift of chocolate truffles and a new Oxford shirt may as well have been mailed into a black hole. But his father also kept cash in tumbleweeds of crumpled bills, all over his apartment. Hidden in coffee cups, in the drawer where he kept his tooth-brush and razor, in the toes of his shoes, bursting out of his pockets like stuffing in a couch. GJ had never gone to his grandfather's be-fore, not without Greg, but it seemed possible he might, if he was desperate.

"Think about it: GJ could easily get there, even if he walked, in a matter of days. Your dad always liked him, his namesake, the heir to the Reinart dynasty . . ." This she said bitterly, her mouth tight, like she'd found a pit in her own words and was looking for a way to spit it out.

"Why don't we just go inside and I'll call him and ask?" Greg put his plate on the dinette. The rock in his gut had ruined every-thing. He didn't want to go back to her condo, no more than she wanted him there, but he liked threatening her with the possibility.

"Sure, we can do that," she said. Always calling his bluff. "We should do that. But I have a feeling you'll still drive over there to see for yourself."

She was right. He had come this far. It'd be the first thing Deb would ask. *Did you check your dad's?* Maybe Deb should have taken this trip. Maybe Marie should have. Instead it was him, bumbling here and there. Jesus, was he even really looking? *Grow a pair.* His mother's voice. He felt her cigarette ashes in his throat.

"I'll drive there first thing," he said. Marie clinked her water glass to his. "This is a good thing. You're doing a good thing," Marie said. She reached across the short distance between them and touched his knee. "You're probably not going to find him. But you're looking for him, and that's what matters. It's a long time coming."

You're probably not going to find him. It was beginning to feel like GJ lived in another dimension, lived in the dream Greg had just had, maybe, but in this one he was just a memory, a conjuring. "What are you going to do?"

"I'm going to wait for him," Marie said. "He knows I'm here. I'm not going down to OBT anymore, and I'm not coming with you to your father's. But I'll stay right here and every day I'll wait for him to knock on the door and ask if we can order Chinese."

It had been a family tradition, when they were a family, to order Chinese every Thursday night. When Greg moved out he'd tried to make pizza Fridays a new tradition, but it never stuck. GJ always wanted Chinese instead.

"I haven't seen my dad in a long time," Greg said.

"You don't like him," Marie said. "You always hated how he stood by and let your mother treat you like shit."

Greg was used to Marie's declarations, her sudden insights, but this was something new.

"And your mother is why you hate women," she went on. "She made you feel insignificant in her life, second to the parties she had, her friends, second to your dad, second second second."

"I don't hate women, Marie." It was her tone, the way she made it sound like a foregone conclusion, something everybody in the world but him already knew. "Just because you and I didn't work out doesn't mean I hate every woman. I just hate you."

He'd meant it to be a joke, but it came out all wrong; he sounded defensive, peevish. He sounded like he meant it.

"Oh, believe me, I've made my peace with that," she said. She reached over and took his plate. "Sometimes I think our destiny was to make GJ. Isn't that a nice way of looking at it? We didn't work out but we created a life. Then sometimes I think destiny is a load of horseshit. Did you see how comfortable everyone seemed last night? How at home? This is the life they choose."

He had forgotten—how easy it was to forget!—how Marie could unload on him, pow pow pow, how she could pour her every thought into his lap and then look at him like he should have brought a towel.

"Can I tell you something else?" She popped the last bit of bagel into her mouth. "Your mom was jealous of you."

He could feel his heart pounding, his face getting hot; he must have looked red and sweaty to her, hugely fat, his bare feet with their yellowing toenails; no matter what he did to stop it everything changed color, shape, his hair his toenails his enormous fat body. He must have looked defeated, even as a small voice inside him told him that wasn't what she was after. Still, he wanted to shout at her, scare her, get in his own blade, right between her ribs, wherever it hurt. It was the same way he had often felt about his mother: unable to find the words, and that if he did find them, he did not have her permission to use them. "I need to shower and get on the road," he said. "I'll call you if I find out anything."

"I'm serious, Greg," she said. "Did you know there are two kinds of people in this world? Those who forgive their parents, and those who don't. GJ does not forgive us. You do not forgive your parents. Your mom was so jealous of you that she couldn't see straight. Your youth, your opportunities, everything she didn't have. Your dad paid her all his attention because he knew it, too. You forget that I knew her. *I knew her*, Greg. Did you know she wanted to be a fashion designer? That was her dream, but then she got married and had you. She was just a sad lady who got in her own way. That's all she was. She failed you and we failed GJ. See how that happens?"

"What do you want me to say?" He wanted to stand, to tower over her, but the maneuvering it took to rise from the dinette bench was something best done in private. He did not want Marie to witness it.

"I want you to understand that sometimes people are just shitty. Even GJ."

"He's your son, too. I don't get how you can talk about him like this. He could be dead."

She winced. Greg felt that old triumph.

"If he is, there's nothing we can do, is there? And if he's not, there's nothing we can do."

"So you're saying that this whole trip is pointless. You're saying that I'm a fool for even trying."

"You already knew that, Greg. It doesn't mean you aren't still *trying*."

"I can't tell if you want to make me feel better or worse," he said.

"I just want you to understand that GJ is who he is. That everyone is who they are. People disappoint you. You've never learned how to deal with disappointment. Deb is the one who came closest but I'm willing to bet she's fed up with you."

It was a roller coaster, talking to Marie. His stomach dropping, his urge to scream, then the calm slow climb up the summit, everything righting itself again, just before another drop.

"Please don't talk about something you know nothing about." Deb had been relieved to see him go. *Relieved*. "Fuck you, Marie."

"And that's my cue," she said. She stood and made her way to the door. "I am grateful to you," she said. "I do think this is important. An important gesture. I'm here if you find anything."

As soon as she was gone, as if to prove something to her, he dialed home. He checked his watch and was alarmed to see it was already ten in the morning; he must have slept in, carried along by the terrible dream, by the strange comfort he found lying next to his son in a coffin. He would be lucky to catch Deb, lucky if she hadn't already bustled out the door for her day full of errands, but she picked up after the fourth ring.

"I was just on my way out," she said. "I saw it was you on the caller ID. Did you find him?"

"No," Greg said. "Marie and I went down to OBT and asked around but he wasn't there, hadn't been there in a while."

"Oh," she said. He heard the grandfather clock sound in the background; it had always been a few minutes off. "What are you going to do now?"

"Might go see my dad," he said.

"You think he's there? Huh."

"No . . . I don't know. He could be, right? He could be anywhere."

"Mm-hmm." She sounded distracted; Greg could picture her snatching a glance at the clock, shifting from foot to foot, impatient to get started with her day.

"I'm sorry I didn't call yesterday evening," he said.

"That's okay. I figured you'd be busy. How is she?" Deb's manners were her armor. Kill them with kindness.

"The same. She's exactly the same," he said. He looked out the passenger-side window for Marie, but she was gone, already back in her condo. Maybe even watching him out the window.

"The more people change, the more they stay the same." Deb laughed, a small-talk kind of laugh, her way of dipping a toe in without wetting the whole foot.

Greg watched a man in flip-flops and a tank top emerge from the dark hallway and shuffle over to his car, a blue Toyota with the spare tire on. Out the back window Greg could see the man staring at the RV, looking around as if to see if anyone else saw what he saw. He shook his head and ducked into the car, which started up with a loud growl.

"I have to go," Greg said. "I have to move the RV because it's parked kind of illegally."

"Okay."

"I'll come home today if you want me to." He hadn't intended on saying it, didn't even mean it, really, but still, he felt himself holding his breath, waiting for Deb to answer. It was getting hot in the RV, sweat running down his back like hot fingertips, gliding right down into the funnel of his buttcrack. He needed to get up, turn the AC on, shower, and drive.

"You do whatever you feel is best," Deb said. "This is your thing. I'm not going to get in the way of it."

"Marie thinks it's a waste of time, too," he said.

"That's not what I said."

"Well," Greg said. The sweat was coming faster now.

"Whatever you decide," she said. If Marie had said these words, they'd have meant a dozen other things, Greg scrambling around for clues like they were grenade pins. But it was clear that Deb truly did not care either way. It did not feel like a good thing.

"I think I will go over to my dad's, then," Greg said.

"Good. I think that's good. It's good to be decisive."

For a moment Greg wanted to ask her if it would be just as good to return home, if she'd even want him there, if she was fed up like Marie said. He thought of the ottoman, the couch, the glitter of dust whirling and falling in the light. There was a framed portrait of a cow above the mantel, a candle that smelled of evergreen on the side table. A bowl of TV remotes. An ass-shaped divot in his favorite chair. In his home with Marie and GJ there had also been things, things that felt like his, a painting of a cornfield, a horseshoe hanging in the kitchen, a dish of peach-scented potpourri in the guest bathroom that one day smelled like nothing. He had become just another object in each home, a depression in a cushion, an odorless pile of debris. Easily removed, forgotten, unnecessary. Was that how GJ felt, too? Was that why it was so hard to conjure him, to envision his face, to *see* where he was? Houses remain houses. It had once felt like good news, a kind of freedom. He wanted a beer now, painfully cold, to slice down his throat in a fizzing cavalcade. And another and another.

"I'll call you in a little while," he said, and they hung up. He was being decisive.

Greg took GJ camping, encouraged by Deb; now that they were living in Greensboro they hardly saw the boy. It was high time for a visit. And Marie had been telling them things. How she came home to a party in the condo when GJ thought she'd be away the whole weekend at a new boyfriend's house. How GJ had apologized, how there were cigarette burns in her curtains, how he'd been *high, Greg, high as a kite* but swore it was just weed. How he'd lost his job at the food court, something about a new manager coming on who had it in for GJ. How he slept all day but was awake all night, like a cat, jittery and talkative and *strange*. How he had only three months to go before graduation but he'd been skipping. Greg listened to all of it over the phone, read her e-mails with their all-caps urgency. It felt like a luxury to him, this period of messiness. Kids did drugs, kids acted out, kids tested their parents' limits. It was all part of it. He hadn't been allowed the same freedom; his mother had kicked him out when he was sixteen for calling her a drunk, had taken him back in only when Mrs. Helen phoned her and said it was time for him to come home. And only then because it embarrassed her, the neighbor knowing the family business. She had come to the door in one of her best suits, hugged him when Mrs. Helen summoned him from her kitchen, where he'd been gripping a cold glass of lemonade, hoping she'd go away. Then at home she had gone back to ignoring him, her silent treatment as thick as the cigarette smoke that trailed her from room to room.

So GJ had it good, in Greg's estimation. He could fuck up all he wanted to, at least for a while. No one would be kicking him out. Instead he would take his son on a camping trip, something they'd done plenty of times back when GJ was a Boy Scout.

He bought a brand-new tent, one with a skylight so they could see the stars from their sleeping bags, which he also bought brand-new: thick, luxuriant cocoons that guaranteed warmth in temperatures as low as fifteen below zero, though they'd be camping in the Panhandle in April. Headlamps; hiking boots (GJ's special-ordered size fifteens); packets of grub in stew, pot pie, and chili flavors; a paperback of ghost stories that was by the register; and a watch for GJ that featured a small compass just above the 6.

He flew in to the Orlando airport, which always felt like a theme park in its own right, dazed parents walking behind children skipping and shrieking and eating sticky lollipops or candy necklaces, expensive shops featuring authentic key lime candies or sugared orange peels or cartoon mouse keychains, everyone moving in a slow herd as the blue sky and white sun poured in through the floor-to-ceiling windows. Being away from central Florida for a time always made Greg feel nostalgic. He moved among the herd feeling loose, relaxed. He wasn't going to Disney World; he wasn't shepherding his exhausted children onto a plane to go back to the dreary gray of Minnesota or the parched Texas landscape. His son was nearly grown; he was taking him on a camping trip, a trip he hoped they'd look back on in the years to come. A trip he hoped would be like a couple of badly needed sutures over the withering wound his relationship with GJ had become. They didn't fight; it was even worse: GJ was polite to him, overly polite, in the same way that the gate agent had called him *sweetheart.* A distant kind of polite, even a pitying kind. But now he was doing something fatherly, something that would bring them closer. He had spent three thousand dollars, all in; his expensive new haul was probably wheeling around baggage claim, just waiting for him to retrieve it and pack it neatly in the trunk of the SUV he rented, GJ's watch zippered snugly in his carry-on.

He got to Marie's in record time, enjoying the drive, the moon roof in the rental open and the wind loosening him up, making him feel wide open. In retrospect, that was the best part of the trip.

He was not prepared for what GJ looked like, not prepared to see his son's cheekbones jutting painfully out from his face, his hair thin and oily, a thick silver earring in his ear, the enormous jeans he was wearing, a single handcuff around his wrist. It had been three months since he'd seen the boy, over Christmas. No earring then, no cheekbones.

"Hey," GJ said, breaking into an easy grin. His gums looked pale, patches of stubble dotting his face. He hugged Greg, and Greg hugged him back, alarmed to feel his son's shoulder blades. He looked at Marie, standing just behind GJ in the kitchen. She mouthed, *I told you.*

GJ pulled back and bent for his bag, a bright orange cross-body that had smudges of dirt and what must have been a hundred safety pins holding together an enormous tear. Greg hadn't bought GJ a new bag; it hadn't even occurred to him, though there had been a whole row of them along the back wall of the store.

"Is that a handcuff?" Greg asked. It was the wrong thing to say, the wrong thing to notice and call out, but he couldn't help it, a *fucking handcuff*?

"Oh," GJ said, looking down at his wrist. As if he'd forgotten it was there. "Yeah, it's not real."

"Huh," Greg said, so that he would not say *Take it off*.

"Bye, Mom," GJ said, and hugged her, a quick one-armed hug, not the two-armed crusher he'd given Greg, and it made Greg want to hug the boy all over again. They walked down the hallway together toward the parking lot, Marie trailing behind.

"Hey," she whispered. Greg slowed so he was walking beside her.

"He just got home. Like an hour ago." Her eyes were red; there were black gashes under them. Greg often finished reading her e-mails or listening to her phone calls feeling skeptical; Marie was an overreactor, an overthinker. But in the hallway looking at her exhausted face he wondered if maybe she had been protecting him, if maybe she hadn't told him enough.

"Where was he?" he whispered.

She shrugged, keeping her eyes on GJ, who was standing in the parking lot now, looking back at them, his body as thin and curved as a sail.

"It's the blue one," Greg called. He pushed the button on the small remote to unlock the doors.

"I think he's still messed up," Marie said. "He's too happy. Sometimes when he comes down he gets sick. He doesn't think I know but of course I know. I just thought you should be prepared."

"Marie," Greg said, louder than he wanted to. He waited for GJ to get into the passenger seat and shut the door. "Maybe we shouldn't be going on this trip at all."

"No, you still should," she said. She backed away from him, moving down the hallway to her door. "You have to. He needs this." She was barefoot, and when she turned to walk the rest of the way he saw that the soles of her feet were dirty, almost black, like she'd been pacing the hallway all night. She locked the door behind her; Greg heard the dead bolt clunk into place.

GJ was resting his head against the window when Greg got into the car, his thumbs tapping his legs, *one-one, one-one*. Greg had imagined a kind of speech he'd give GJ before they set off, something about how GJ was nearly a man and should be able to find his way in the world and to get there on time, and then hand the watch over in a small front-seat ceremony before suggesting McDonald's or Beefy King. But that could wait, all of it could wait. The main thing was to get them there, to point the SUV north and set up camp.

"Are you hungry?" he asked, keeping his voice quiet; he knew all too well what a hangover felt like. "We could get egg sandwiches."

"Hey, Dad?" GJ unbuckled himself and pulled the door handle. "Just hold on one sec, okay?" One sec. Classic GJ. He'd started using the phrase as a child, maybe four or five, after hearing Marie or Greg use it. It had become a family joke. *Just one sec!* Greg started to laugh, started to feel grateful to his son for invoking such a treasure, but he stopped when GJ bent over, his spine jutting through his T-shirt, and vomited onto the asphalt. Greg heard it splash as it landed, GJ burping and coughing in an oddly businesslike way, like it was something he just had to get through, spitting and sighing when he was done.

"Sorry about that, Dad," he said. He opened the flap of his bag and pulled out a pack of gum, holding it out to Greg first. "I don't know what it is. Something must be going around. But I feel better now."

Again Greg fought the urge to stop the entire trip, to lead GJ by his elbow back into Marie's condo, fly back to Greensboro, and return everything he'd bought, even the watch.

"Hey," Greg said. He grabbed GJ by the arm, squeezing hard. "It's enough of this shit, okay? Your mom and I, we're done putting up with this." Tough love, he just needs a little tough love. That's what Deb was always saying. "It's time for you to grow up."

GJ looked at him, right into his eyes. His whole life he'd had eyes that looked heartbroken, searching, as innocent as a child's. "I know," he said. He wiped his mouth with the back of his hand. "I just need to get it together." Later Greg would be able to see how expertly GJ would take what he'd just said and repeat it in a new way, making it seem like he was truly listening, that it was all sinking in. But that day in the car, with the camping gear practically radiating newness, a fresh start from the backseat, his son's pale gaunt face and his sick wet mouth, Greg felt like he'd done something right. He'd gotten through.

"I just want to have a good weekend with you," GJ said. "It's all out of my system now. McDonald's sounds great." But he didn't eat the sandwich Greg got him; he held it, half-open, in his lap and threw it away at a rest stop fifty miles down the road.

GJ slept for most of the drive, waking up when he needed to pee and then falling back into a heavy, head-lolling sleep. It felt like a mercy to Greg, no need to make small talk, no way he could ask the same question he'd asked already, or the wrong question, no way to trigger a batch of awkward silence he'd been dreading since the day he bought the tent.

He pulled into the campground a little past eight in the evening. At the entrance a woman in a wide-brimmed hat took Greg's credit card, handed it back to him with a complimentary brick of soap. "We make it ourselves," she said, but Greg couldn't tell who *we* was; she was alone in the small guard's cabin that looked like all it housed was a lopsided office chair and a desk the size of a Bible. He placed the soap in the glove compartment and only remembered it was in there on the plane back to Greensboro.

He and GJ made camp in a clearing about a mile in and went to bed immediately, GJ zipped all the way into his sleeping bag, just the angular planes of his face showing. Greg pulled open the flap to the skylight, cringing at the loud scrape of the Velcro, though GJ didn't stir. Greg lay back and looked up. Soon, despite the sour smell coming off his son, despite his twitching, despite the fact that Greg had no idea who this skeletal being was, had maybe never known, had taken it for granted that he had time to get to know him, that he wouldn't change into someone else, shape-shift into an *other*, bury his true self in a sleeping bag, despite Greg knowing that after the weekend, after the hiking and the brief plunge into the icy lake and the twenty minutes GJ wandered into the trees and came back smiling and the twenty minutes after that when he was vomiting again and the cold stew and cold chili and cold tuna sandwiches and cold coffee and cold hot dogs, everything cold, the whole trip so freezing that they ground their jaws when they spoke to stop the chattering, the warm tent and warm sleeping bags and the way GJ said, *This was fun, Dad,* in as sincere a voice as Greg had ever heard, despite Greg knowing that after all that GJ would still be in trouble and that it was likely his fault, he'd fucked the boy up, he wasn't his mother but he'd fucked the boy up regardless, despite all of that, when he thought back on it on the plane home and in the days afterward, it all felt worth it. His son asleep next to him. The cocoon of his sleeping bag, both of them safe and warm. The papering of stars glowing down from the tent skylight. How they twinkled like jewels. Like burst glass, tumbling across the tar.

The highway heading to his dad's felt cozy, intimate, walled in by the trees on each side, a neatly mown median dividing the four lanes, the sky like a fuzzy gray lid. He'd showered, the RV tank's water puttering meekly down onto his head and shoulders, and then drove out of the parking lot at Marie's condo with wet hair and wet feet and the soap he hadn't had enough water to wash off sliming his balls. It itched him now, and it felt good to be alone so he could scratch and scratch without a disappointed, sighing *Oh, honey* coming from Deb. He'd eaten three egg biscuits, and now he was nursing the last of his sweet tea, which got sweeter and sweeter the more he drank.

He had power of attorney for his dad; he knew the man's finances as well as his own. Why he chose to live in a shithole in his declining years was a mystery. He could afford at-home care and he could afford to live in one of those swanky high-rises where people start at the top floors and move toward the bottom the less able they become. Greg had explained both options to him thoroughly when it became obvious his father needed help. But he'd chosen to be in an assisted-living community set back off a busy road in what felt like a dorm room to Greg, though he'd only visited twice. Thin walls, thin carpeting. Dingy mini-blinds. Food people had been encouraged to stop eating since the '80s. It would have made his mother ill, a place like that; Greg could picture her clutching one of her crystal ashtrays and shaking her head no no no the way she did at the end. She had ruled with an iron fist when she was alive, Greg's father silently going along. In fact, that was his legacy, in Greg's eyes. A long trail of silence. All he could think was that it was some final act of defiance on his dad's part, this betrayal of what his wife would have wanted if she'd lived to die with him. That or the old man had become even stingier in his waning years.

He pulled off the highway and coasted onto the main road. BP, Chevron, Popeye's, Subway, Pizza Hut, McDonald's on each side and one farther up ahead if his eyes weren't playing tricks. He wasn't hungry but he could eat. He could bring his father lunch. He stopped for a sack of tacos at the Taco Bell and a quick shit in what ended up being a surprisingly clean bathroom. Not a stray wing of toilet paper to be seen. The smell of bubble gum and soap. The achingly white clean bowl. It felt like a gift, a good omen.

He rang the buzzer outside his dad's door, a featureless wood plank that had been painted brown to match the brown shutters nailed outside each window. There was a wreath hanging on the door that said *Friends Welcome*. Not something his father would have purchased for himself. It was likely something each resident had been given at Christmas or something, though he didn't see one on any of the other doors. His dad opened the door, looked up at Greg through the shrubs of hair above each eye. He was more stooped than he had been the last time Greg saw him, but the old man had a clean shirt tucked into pressed gray pants and fresh white sneakers. His usual handkerchief poking a corner out of his breast pocket: turquoise, today, an odd vividness that Greg wanted to shake his head no no no at.

Greg held up the tacos. "Hey, Dad," he said.

"I can't eat that," his father said, stepping aside so Greg could pass. "Ulcers."

"Oh, that's right," Greg said. "I'm sorry—I can go out and get something else?"

"I already ate. They make us eat at noon like kindergartners." His father closed the door, the darkness in the apartment closing around them. It had been so bright outside, and Greg blinked, looking around, waiting for everything to take shape. Finally the small round dining table appeared, and then the rest of the kitchen. He set his lunch on the table, suddenly feeling self-conscious about eating it. He knew his father couldn't eat fast food. He *knew* that. He'd purchased eight tacos anyway. The bag hummed, whispered, pulled at him. He turned his back on it.

"I didn't know you were coming," his dad said. He lowered himself into a worn blue easy chair, crossed one knee over the other. Greg sat on the small sofa across from him, a card table between them with the day's newspaper scattered across it.

"It was sort of last minute," Greg said. "We're not sure where GJ has gone off to." He heard himself trying to make it seem like it wasn't a big deal, nothing to worry about. Over the years he hadn't told his dad much about GJ's troubles. What was the point? His father couldn't do anything; he didn't want to be disturbed during the twilight years of his life. Greg also didn't want his father to have anything over him. To know he'd messed up, botched it, made a mockery of fatherhood when it was all so simple: just go to work and come home. Hugs on birthdays and graduation. Back into the shadows when there are tears or raised voices. Don't divorce; that is an option only for the weak. His father knew enough. Did he really need to know about all the times GJ fell off the wagon? About the two times he'd been arrested? About the fourteen months he spent in jail? No. He didn't need to know any of it.

"You're not sure where your son is?" His father uncrossed his leg, leaned forward with his elbows on his knees. His face was Greg's face minus one million beers, minus all those cream cakes and pizzas and whiskey. The same pummeled nose, though: that swollen purple blossom with its tiny infrastructure of capillaries. His wrists poked out of his shirt cuffs as white as cream.

"That's about the extent of it," Greg said. He felt the need to keep the conversation concise, businesslike. His father's attention span had always been short, shorter still for anything that bored or potentially overwhelmed him. Best to state the facts and be done with it. "I dropped by to see you and to see if maybe you'd seen him. Or heard from him."

"I haven't seen him in years. But he did call me, not too long ago. I'll have to check my log." Greg's father gripped the arms of the chair and pushed himself up, stumbling a bit. Greg reached up and caught him, the man's arm as delicate as a wing in Greg's hand. "Thank you. I'll just be a minute."

His log. Greg's father recorded the details of his day in a lined journal and had done so for as far back as Greg could remember. He stored the logs in bookshelves, and then boxes, and now they lived in the storage unit Greg paid for via an auto-deduction from his account every six months, along with his mother's things. Greg flipped through them from time to time, looking for anything interesting, some clue as to the kind of man his father truly was, but they said things like *Ate egg for breakfast with a bit of black pepper. Saw bird at park. Had tire inspected.* Volume after volume of the basic facts of a man's life. The sparser, the better. Greg counted and divided and catalogued. His father listed what he knew to be true. *Today is Tuesday.*

"Here it is," his father said. His journal looked like a sheath of lined paper kids used in school, with three staples binding it on the left side. "He called me just last week, on Wednesday."

"Are you sure?" Greg asked. His heart felt like someone had attached a tire pump to it. Inflated and buoyant. Terrified. Last Wednesday was only two days before he'd left to find GJ, and now it was Sunday.

"It's what I wrote down," his father said, pointing at the page. He handed the journal over to Greg. It felt damp and he could see that some of the ink was smeared, his father likely having spilled the glass of water he put his teeth in across the pages. The entry read *Hot outside today. Took a nap in the afternoon. Greg Junior called, and we talked for nearly eight minutes.*

"What did you talk about?" Greg asked. Eight minutes was a lifetime.

"It doesn't say," his father said.

"Yes, but can you try to remember?"

His father sat in the chair again, closed his eyes as he thought. "We talked about how hot it has been." He kept his eyes closed, like a medium channeling a spirit. "Hotter than usual. He said he was somewhere even hotter, or he'd been somewhere like that recently. He asked me for money and I said he'd have to come by and get it, but he never did. It's still in that envelope on the table."

Greg went over to the envelope. Inside were twenties and a couple fifties. Probably a thousand dollars in there. Maybe fifteen hundred.

"You have to stop keeping cash around the apartment like this," Greg said. "And giving GJ this kind of money won't help him." The sharp, comforting smell of onions wafted from the bag on the table. Greg unwrapped a taco and took a bite, catching what dribbled onto his chin with his knuckles. It smelled better than it tasted, the cheese going cold, the meat flabby in its own stale juices, the shell worn through with grease.

"Have you called his friends? Or Marie?" His father often ignored the financial advice Greg gave him; if he hadn't had power of attorney his father would have withdrawn all the money he could and shoved it, bill by bill, under his bed.

"I just came from Marie's. We went downtown and asked around. No dice."

"Maybe he's still on his way here."

"Maybe," Greg said. Wednesday. Wednesday. What had happened since that day? Why had he called his grandfather and not Greg? He heard a toilet flush. He thought it was from the resident next door and was about to lament to his father for the hundredth time how thin the walls were when an old woman walked out of his father's room wearing a pale pink robe.

"This is Lydia," his father said.

"Hello," the woman said. She walked toward Greg with her small, tan hand out.

"Lyd, this is my son, Greg."

"Greg! Another Greg," she said. She grasped his hand in hers, the small claw of a bird. "We have four Gregs in this community."

She was younger than his dad, maybe even a decade younger. Her hair looked more silver than white, loosely curled and windblown. Bedhead, Greg realized. It was bedhead because she'd slept in his father's bed, his bony old dad with his paper-thin flesh and watery eyes and wet mouth. She pressed his hand between her thumb and fingers and released him.

"Your father never mentioned me, I'm presuming?" She arched her eyebrows at Greg's dad and then at him, mock scolding. She had no idea that Greg's dad hadn't mentioned her because Greg's dad never mentioned anything, and because Greg did not call him. "Is that food I smell?" She drifted past Greg, over to the table where the sack lay in a lump. She unwrapped a taco halfway and took a bite, working the food in her mouth in the complicated, cudlike way of people with dentures.

"Greg's son—my grandson—has gone missing," his father said.

Greg had not put it that way, had in fact gone out of his way to not put it that way.

"Are you shitting me?" the woman asked. She wiped her mouth on the sleeve of her robe. She was alternately graceful and un-mannered, Greg was gathering. She had pale violet eyes and a small queen's face. "We have to find him."

"That's what I'm trying to do," Greg said. Had she been the one to put up the wreath? Did she live here? He looked around for further evidence of her, but there was none that he could see. "He's an adult with past . . . issues, so involving the police isn't really an option. He might just be somewhere we can't reach him." He had meant that to sound like good news, but the woman looked at him with her eyebrows up like he'd just offered the possibility that GJ was dead.

"Dad here says he talked to him just last Wednesday, too. So that's a promising clue," he said, but Lydia's eyebrows did not go back down.

"Did he, now?" she said. She folded the wrapper back over her taco and shoved it in the bag. "You know, sometimes your father gets his days messed up." Greg looked at his dad, who was listening to Lydia talk with a small smile on his face. "Wednesday last week might mean Wednesday last year. Isn't that right, Greg?"

His dad chuckled. "I guess so," he said. She was talking about him like he was a child, like the man part of him wasn't present. She was talking about him the way Greg's mother always had. Greg had chosen Deb for how unlike Marie she was: unfailingly calm, unwounding, unwounded. He had run toward her corner like the corner Marie was in was spitting acid. That clearly hadn't been his father's tactic. His father, it turned out, missed the burn.

"Dad," Greg said. He waited for his father to look at him. "It had to be last week, right? Because of the money on the table. If it was last year you wouldn't have put the money on the table, right?"

"You'd be surprised," Lydia said, and laughed, a throaty *haw haw haw* that made Greg like her, despite also feeling like she was getting in the way. Scrambling his father's signal.

"What were we doing last Wednesday, G?" She looked at Greg's father, who shrugged. "Was that the night we took the shuttle to dinner?" She turned to Greg. "The shuttle is a smelly van contraption that takes us residents on errands and out for dates, but only when there are enough people to fill each seat. The driver gets paid by the passenger." She rolled her eyes and adjusted the sash on her robe. The bit of her chest that was peeking through was mottled and tanned and sexless, like the breast of a roast chicken. "I think that was the night," she said. "We went to Panera. Then we came home and watched *Wheel of Fortune*, and then we hmm hmm hmm . . ." She winked at Greg, as if he would delight in hearing that his father wasn't too fragile to perform, and in fact he did feel a small bit of happiness for his father, and happiness for himself, if he'd live to be as old as the old man. "Oh, and then you got a phone call! You did! You got a phone call."

"I told you," his father said. He was tired, his mouth slack, his eyes half-closed. It used to bother Greg, how around his parents he reverted to feeling like a child, petulant and voiceless. But now he was glad for it. For days, years maybe, he'd felt old, heavy, shabby. But he was a young man, compared with this decrepit shit-hole and its papery inhabitants, a cheap dollhouse and its cheap dolls. He was the midpoint between GJ and his father, caretaker for both. If only they'd let him. "I write everything down," his father said, closing his eyes.

"Yes, we know," Lydia said. She glided into the kitchen, her bare heels peeking out from under the long robe, like small brown dinner rolls. Bare feet and a robe. She was definitely at home here. His father already had a glistening of drool gathered in his lower lip.

"Greg," Lydia hissed. "Come in here."

She was filling the old ceramic teapot of his mother's with water from the tap. "I'm going to make some tea," she whispered. "Do you want?"

"No thanks," he whispered back. His father used to drink Ovaltine every morning; that's what Greg wanted, though it felt more like Lydia's kitchen, not his father's. Not a kitchen where he could feel comfortable searching the cabinets.

"So," Lydia said, using her normal voice now. "Is he a user, this boy of yours?"

"What?" Greg whispered.

"I have one of my own," she said. "My daughter. She's proba-bly about your age."

Greg looked at her, not sure how to answer.

"A drug addict," she said, enunciating so thoroughly that Greg could see the line where her dentures met her gums. "They're real assholes, aren't they?"

"Your daughter is my age and she's a drug addict?" He wasn't sure he understood her correctly. In all the years since GJ had been the way he was, Greg always figured he'd get it together one day. Get a job, a place of his own. Grow up. On the TV shows, the addicts were told over and over that if they didn't stop, they'd die. It seemed like a given: Stop if you want to live. Use if you want to die. Lydia's drug addict daughter was *his* age? Nearly sixty?

"Well, I should say she goes between drugs and drink. When she drinks she can at least hold a job. When it's the other thing sometimes I don't hear from her for a while." She held the teapot over the stove, like she was trying to decide which burner. Finally she dropped it carelessly onto the one closest to her. Everything she did was loud, Greg was starting to realize. Unapologetic. "But old people rarely hear from their families, anyway," she said, winking. "One day you'll stop letting it get to you." She turned the heat up on the burner, then leaned her hip into the counter. A younger woman's pose. He wondered what she was like when it was getting to her. The not seeing her daughter. The not knowing.

"My wife and I, my ex-wife and I, we went to a part of town where GJ likes to go," Greg said. He felt drawn in by this woman, opened up, like he couldn't tell her everything fast enough. "We went to a place where bad things happen. Ugly things. My ex-wife says people go there by choice." He thought of how he'd gone there by choice, all those years ago. How the woman had gotten down and crawled, scrabbling under the bar like a rodent. How he hadn't been able to see her when she took him into her mouth.

"Free will," Lydia said. "God gave us free will." She raised a tan claw above her head, like she had the answer in class, then brought it down into a clap. "Assholes." The teapot whined quietly, like a wounded animal trying to stay hidden. "I bet you tried some tough love. Am I right?"

Greg nodded.

"Haw. And I bet you've seen your fair share of rehab joints. Listen." She grabbed his arm, little pincers working into the flesh. "At some point it can't be your fault anymore. Maybe it used to be your fault. But it's not anymore." The teapot pitched higher, really letting loose now. Greg cut his eyes at it, hoping it'd signal her, but she dug in harder. "The day you understand that is the day you'll truly be free." She released him and snapped off the burner, the teapot's shriek exhaling from a whine to a sigh. "Like me," she said.

"You feel free," he said. "What if something happens? What if she disappears? Our son has never done anything like this before."

"You're not listening," she said. She wound the string from her tea bag around the handle of a mug. "I just told you that it's not your fault anymore. Are you dropping little bags of dope down onto his head when he's sleeping? Are you driving him to that ugly place and pushing him out of the car? Yes, you were probably a shitty father in a lot of ways. Guess what. I told my daughter every year on her birthday that she was too fat. Her dad left me for his secretary. Her stepdad was a child-toucher. I kicked her stepdad out and changed the locks. Do you know how many times I apologized for it all? Maybe it matters, but it doesn't matter enough. Eventually you have to let go."

My problem isn't that I can't let go, Greg wanted to say. *It's that I never held on.* The trip he was on, that was his way of holding on, but it was still all wrong. Maybe it would matter, but would it matter enough?

"Jean over in one-F told me she used to put her baby's hand on a hot burner so he'd learn not to touch it. She told me that like she was proud of it, how clever!" She blew into her mug. "Your own dad," she whispered, "told me that he coupled with half the ladies on your block when you were a kid."

"What?" Greg's father had looked at his mother like she was a movie star. Like he was in awe and a bit shy around her. Led her around by the elbow all the way until the end.

"You know how it was back then."

He didn't. His mother had *ruled the roost* was how she always put it. She was beautiful. Half the ladies on the block . . . Mona, in her polyester pantsuits? Mrs. Helen, who always wore a kerchief on her head? When he'd lived there after getting kicked out he saw her without it. Her hair was so thin at her hairline that she looked bald there. Had his father seen her without the kerchief, too?

"I'm saying," Lydia said, "that no one is perfect. We're all human and our children are human. Free"—she snapped her fingers—"will." She snapped them again. Marie had told him people either forgave their parents or they didn't. Lydia was basically telling him the same thing. He was surrounded by people telling him to give up.

"I think it's admirable, what you're doing," she said. She waved her hand around. "You know, and all that." She looked across the counter at the back of his father's sleeping head. "He's a good man," she whispered. "But a shyster, too. People aren't always all one thing."

"I never understood why he chose to live here," Greg said. "Out of all the other places he could have gone."

"That's easy," she said. "It's because this is where I live. Me and all the rest of his girlfriends." She laughed and walked past him to go sit next to his father. "He's awake!" she said. "Probably been listening this whole time."

Greg walked the thirteen steps from the kitchen to the sofa and sat across from them.

"What do you think you'll do now?" Lydia asked. She patted his father's leg, *slap slap slap*. Driving here, Greg had imagined either finding GJ or, the more likely option, taking the old man out for a meal, treating him to Red Lobster, something like that.

"I don't know," he said. "I might drive back home."

Lydia nodded; she approved. "Get back to your life. Your son will turn up. They always do." *Do they?* he wanted to ask.

"I live here because it's a short drive to the range," his father said, his voice graveled with sleep. "You always think people do things just to piss you off." He looked at Greg, his face placid, just a simple fact he was stating. "I just wanted to play golf. Now I can't play golf anymore."

"That's true," Lydia said. She looked at her own knees, shaking her head, bringing her mug up to sip from it.

"It was your mother who always fussed about how things looked. I never cared all that much. I just need a bed and some walls."

"All the comforts of home," Lydia said, patting his leg and winking at Greg again. Was it a grandmotherly wink? An innuendo wink? Again he felt like an intruder. His father had his own life here, a bed and walls and the company of this strange hawk of a woman. Had she been joking about the other girlfriends? His dad seemed exhausted; maybe she hadn't been joking. The years he'd lived with his father were a fraction of the total years he'd lived so far. When it came right down to it his father was no more than an old roommate, someone he tiptoed around and was glad to be rid of. He guessed the feeling was mutual.

He'd always liked GJ, though. *You're named after me, not your father*, Greg's dad would often say. GJ had a solid golf swing;

Greg's was inconsistent at best, too powerful, smashing the ball beyond the green nine times out of ten. GJ was more patient, back when they still visited Greg's father, back before GJ's eyes slid around like they were trying to get away from his head.

"Did Lydia tell you she tried it once?" Greg's father asked.

"Golf?"

"I think he means dope," she said. "Right, Gregory, is that what you meant?"

"Right, right. Tell him."

"Well, one day I decided to kind of give in and see what it was all about." She put her tea on the card table, thought better of it, and put it on the floor by her feet. "My daughter was in one of her dope phases, so I went over there and told her we were going to do it together. Crack, she liked crack. Likes, I guess. We had to go into her closet so her landlord wouldn't smell it. That was about maybe ten years ago now."

"She smoked *crack*," Greg's father said. "And lived to tell the tale!"

"It tasted like a burning foot. But honestly it was wonderful, once it kicked in." She looked at Greg, her eyes shining now. "Maybe that's why it's so easy for me to let go. I know what it feels like. We stayed in that closet for hours. When it was all over I felt foolish, like I'd let her see me get a pap smear or something, but I also felt like I understood her better." For a moment, he recognized the look on Lydia's face. A mixture of pride and sadness. Then she shook herself. "I told her she was an idiot for doing it and I left and we didn't speak for three years. Tough love, haw!"

Greg felt impatient. There had to be more to the story. "I don't get it—why would you want to smoke crack with your own daughter? And are you saying I should be doing drugs with my son? Dad?"

His father moved his feet like he was marching in place, waved his hands in the air like he was trying to bat mosquitoes away. Like Greg was a mosquito. "You're not listening," the old man said.

"I'm tired of people telling me I'm not listening!" Greg yelled. Here it was, the inevitable resurfacing of his childhood self. He had been trying to hold it in but there it sprung, the jackass in the box. "I heard you," he said, trying to sound calmer, though his voice shook and whined. "You"—he pointed at Lydia—"are telling me I should give up and/or smoke crack with my son. And you"—he pointed at his dad—"were about to hand over an envelope of cash to a boy who would only spend it on more drugs. Tell me again how I wasn't listening."

"He's not a *boy*," his father said.

"I'm not telling you to give up," Lydia said. "You see this?" She held her hands up to her face like an awards show presenter. Her cheeks were wet with tears. "I didn't give up. I just moved on."

"I wanted Lydia to tell that crack story so you wouldn't feel so bad about driving around looking for your son in the two most obvious places I can think of. Especially when you could have just called ahead and not wasted your time. Lydia smoked crack with her daughter." She snickered; her emotions were baffling to Greg, shooting out in every direction, the way the water shot out of the calcified showerhead in his bathroom back home. "You drove down to Florida. Neither of you had any better ideas. It's all just a shot in the dark."

"What do you think I should do?" Greg asked, no longer trying to disguise the peevishness in his voice.

Lydia and his father stared at him, Lydia's eyes wide and almost luridly violet through the tears, his father's drooping and lashless.

"I don't know," Greg's father finally said. "Call hospitals and jails. Go home and wait by the phone. Or maybe you can throw a dart at a map like they do in the movies. Hell, maybe that's what GJ did."

"He said he was coming here, though," Greg said, but he trailed off. His heart wasn't in it. He was only seventy percent certain the phone call had happened, and that it had been GJ on the other end. Sixty percent. The envelope of cash could have been rent, could have been payment to Lydia for services rendered; the mean thought felt good as it passed through his mind. Maybe she took her dentures out. Maybe she talked dirty. Deb had read an article once that said STDs were rampant in retirement communities. *The women leave a scarf tied around their doorknob*, she'd said. *And that means they're open for business.* They'd laughed and Greg had said something like *Good for them!* Now he felt annoyed by the thought. He and Deb built up to sex in a series of elaborate steps: first she showered, and then he did. Sometimes he just went in and shut the door and let the water run while he sat on the toilet, watching the dark trees beyond the frosted window bend and sway, like some kind of dance performance. He'd wet his hair in the sink, run a washcloth over his balls. Then he'd get into his boxers and T-shirt while Deb lotioned her hands and wrists for what felt like hours. Then they lay next to each other, holding hands. Then a hammering of pecking kisses. Fifty pounds ago, he would have moved himself on top of her once he'd begun kissing her neck. But now Deb had to straddle him, working her bent leg over his body like she was mounting a camel for the very first time, each shifting and apologizing. Then the silent, almost ritualistic pumping. Inevitably, Deb would ask, *Are we there yet?* Which was his cue to get there. Deb treated sex like a chore she enjoyed finishing and finishing well, but a chore nonetheless. She could get a dish to shine and squeak, but what did it do for her? Greg had often wondered what, aside from a sense of accomplishment, sex did for her. When they'd first begun dating there had been trips to St. Petersburg, Destin, Savannah, and those trips had involved a lot of eating and a lot of fucking. Fucking, that's what was missing from the sex they had now. Maybe it was because fucking was what you did with a stranger, someone you were getting to know. There was room for surprise, shock, even. Now he and Deb knew each other well. And here his father was, fucking strangers, letting them wear his mother's robe and boil water in his mother's teapot.

But the truth was, after years of chaos, years of the push-pull with Marie and the terror of what GJ was doing to himself, he had brought this calm upon himself. He had drawn it up and over him like a quilt. Hard to breathe under there, sometimes.

"If he comes here," Lydia was saying, "we can just call you. I can hide in the bathroom with my Samsung, lickety-split. Unless you want to stay here and wait," she said, looking down into her mug. It wasn't a real offer, Greg knew.

"No room," Greg's father said. He ran a finger back and forth under his nose. His nails were long and rounded, as if they'd been filed. His fingers and hands looked preserved, cared for, as if they were soaked in formaldehyde and taken out only to be manicured and petted. It made Greg feel queasy, looking at those nails. Another sign that his father was someone he barely knew.

"Don't worry, Dad, I'm heading out." He could go back to the Taco Bell. They had Dr Pepper there, he saw. He could get a large, hell, an extra-large, and if they had it, could add a wedge of lemon, an old trick of Deb's that made the drink taste like one big swallow of sunshine.

"It was so nice to meet you," Lydia said, though they were all still sitting. Greg stood and leaned over to shake her hand again. "You're just exactly like your father." She winked again. Greg wanted to tell her that she was going overboard, she was being too obvious, but then she winked once more and he wondered if she just had a facial twitch.

"Glad you came by, son," Greg's father said. He rose up and gripped Greg's upper arms in what was supposed to be a hug. Greg returned the gesture. His father's arms felt like dowels nestled in wet dough. This was the man who felt like a ghost in the house, a presence they could overlook until it'd been conjured or enraged. The man who sometimes made Greg jog by the open window of the car, around and around the block until the sun had dissolved, losing its fight with the blue and then the gray and then the navy dark, Greg wishing his father would just go back to ignoring him. *Come on, son*, his dad yelling. *Still got a quarter tank left.* His father was one reason freedom for Greg felt like a stack of moon pies and a rocking chair.

"Me, too," Greg said.

Outside, a man in polyester shorts was up on his toes, peering in through the passenger-side window. When he caught sight of Greg he said, "You can't do that. The residents come in here and it's hard enough to pull their cars into the spots they've been assigned, and then here you are just parking wherever you please, and taking up not one, not two, but three spots." The man had his hands on his hips, his thick hairy arms forming two triangles.

"Guess what," Greg said, pulling himself into the driver's seat. He was still thinking of his father's weak, deflated arms, of how his own lungs felt scorched after those evening runs. "I can do whatever the fuck I want."

Greg did get a Dr Pepper, handing the young man an entire five-dollar bill and not waiting for change. A plastic container of lemons rested in a bowl of ice. He took two, tonging them out of the container and into his extra-large cup, so yellow! He would drive home, he decided. Back to Deb and the house and his six hundred cable channels. But first he would stop in Orlando and file a police report. He wouldn't leave until they let him do something official. It was enough, this constant presupposing and searching and protecting. If GJ was doing something illegal, then he deserved to get caught. If he was in trouble, then the cops could help him. It was a win-win.

"Sir," the young man called. He was waving a couple bills in the air. "Please take your change. We aren't allowed to keep tips." The people in line stared at Greg as if he'd left a turd instead of a tip. He took the money and pushed it down into his pocket, the change slapping his leg every step he took out the door. Despite the minor embarrassment, Greg felt hopeful and determined. Like he was finally leveling with himself.

He blew a flat just before I-75 met up with I-4. At first he thought he'd hit something, some kind of animal caught tumbling in his axle, or a cardboard box stuck in his wheel well—that had happened to him once before. The RV sagged to the right side, bumbling down the road, and Greg saw black flaps flying out from behind him, a red Honda swerving and honking and flashing its lights in his side mirror.

"Mother*fucker*," Greg said. He slowed and pulled to the shoulder. When he got out he could see a trail of tire behind him, so many scraps that he was surprised it was only one tire that blew. It was loud out there, the hot wind blasting grit and gnats and exhaust into his face. He stood with his hands on his hips, watching the cars go by, the semis gliding past in a roar. He and Deb had let the AAA membership lag; they hadn't taken a road trip together in years. He had declined the extra roadside assistance package at the RV rental place. He was over a day's drive from home; he was an hour and a half from his father and an hour and a half from Marie. He flipped his cell phone open. He had a three percent charge left. He could call Deb, but what could she do from there? It had to be Marie. He found her number and pressed SEND.

"Guess what," he said when she answered.

"By the sound of it, I'm going to guess you're caught in a tornado, or you ran into some car trouble," she said. Her voice sounded small, nearly engulfed by the din of the highway.

"I'm on I-75 about two miles from I-4," he said.

"I'll be there in an hour," she said, and hung up.

The tow truck showed up first, veering off the road and driving across the median toward Greg like it meant to run him over. Greg had been sitting in the cab of the RV, the AC on blast. He had thought of calling Deb, and then his phone had blinked off and died, making the decision for him.

The tow truck honked and Greg waved, but the driver didn't wave back. He looked around the RV, wondering what he should bring with him, deciding on nothing. Marie was driving across the median now, slower than the tow truck. Greg wondered if he should get out and stop traffic for her, help her get across to where the RV was parked, some way of thanking her for taking care of things. Instead she gunned it, lurching out of the median and across the two lanes, cars honking in her wake. Greg opened the door and climbed down as gracefully as he could. The heat seemed to grow up from the asphalt, reaching up and wiping its hands from the top of Greg's head down to his feet.

Marie rolled down her window and leaned out. "I'll wait in the car," she yelled, then mouthed it again for good measure. Greg gave her the thumbs-up.

The tow truck driver was standing by the RV's rear bumper, writing on a clipboard. His body looked like a belted mattress; Greg wondered how he fit in his truck, how he fit in anything at all.

"This a rental?" the driver asked.

"Yeah," Greg said. "I've been on the road, looking for my son . . ."

"Well," the driver said, "I can tow you to the garage and they can fix your tire there. Two hundred for the tow and probably about the same for the tire. But I gotta warn you, all of these tires are real worn down, so if you put one new tire on and don't re-place the rest, that's going to cause an imbalance down the road."

"An imbalance," Greg repeated.

"That's right," the driver said, going back to his clipboard.

"It's a rental . . . ," Greg said. It came out like a question, Greg unable to control the upward tilt of his voice, the hope that this man wouldn't see how tired he was, how vulnerable and ridiculous.

"Even rentals get run down. Up to you. Either way, it'll be at least twenty-four hours." The driver held his clipboard out to Greg, pointed at where to sign. "The phone number and address are on this." He tore off the top sheet and walked back to his truck.

"Greg," Marie shouted. She waved him over. "He doesn't need you to stand there watching him," she said when Greg was at her window. She wore sunglasses, the frames apple-shaped and enormous.

"I thought I was supposed to help him load it up," Greg said.

"He doesn't need you to do that, either." He felt grateful to Marie; she had called the tow truck and driven an hour to fetch him, and now she was stopping him from making a fool of himself, but despite all of that Greg couldn't help fantasizing bringing his knee up and dislodging her side mirror, watching it tumble to the ground. "Get in," she said, already rolling up her window.

The quiet inside the Buick felt like a blessing. Greg's face relaxed, everything settling back into its place now that he didn't need to squint in the cool darkness. Marie had the radio on low, a man singing *And if I had those golden dreams of my yesterdays . . .*

"This was our wedding song," Greg blurted. It surprised him, the memory so close, like his own hand in front of his face in the darkness, the light suddenly snapped on. Marie's yellow dress, her vanilla perfume oil. Dancing at the bar afterward. *Feel like makin' love . . .* He hadn't meant to say it out loud, hadn't meant to conjure the memory. It was just suddenly there, undeniable.

Marie turned the radio down lower. "So you always claimed," she said. She pulled off the shoulder, lurched onto the highway in a cloud of dust.

"The man said it'll be at least twenty-four hours," Greg said. "You could drop me off at a motel . . ." Again there was the questioning lilt, again the hope.

"How come you were on I-75?" Marie asked. "You should have gotten on I-95 miles ago."

"I was going to file a police report back in town," he said. "Then I was going to head home." He'd forgotten his Dr Pepper; he'd been nursing it until it had melted into a lemony sweetness. He missed it.

"Were you going to tell me about it first?"

"Why would I?" Greg asked. He did his best to keep his voice level, keep it a lemony sweetness.

"Okay," she said. "You know, I'm actually glad this happened. I didn't feel like we had closure when I left your RV this morning."

That was this morning? It seemed impossible. Time was stretching and retracting like the sunlight was just a pale whip of taffy on the pull. He'd been at his father's for what felt like a week's time, but it had truly been about forty-five minutes. He'd wasted the whole day driving, stopping only to argue with people he'd chosen and not chosen to be his family.

Closure. His father hadn't even gotten up to walk him to the door. He wanted to tell Marie that the only closure was death, oblivion. The void. Maybe GJ had found closure. He wanted to argue with Marie. She walked around like she was right, knew everything, saw everything. Even when she was wrong, she found a way to see the light, to become right.

"I meant what I said, though." She put on her blinker and aimed the Buick at the exit for I-4. "I meant everything I said. But it still felt like unfinished business. And then you blew your tire, and here you are."

"Here I am," Greg said. He was trying so hard to keep his voice level that his throat hurt. "There's a La Quinta right off the exit, if you want to take me there," he said. "Or a Homewood Suites across the street. Either way." He'd seen them as he got on the highway that morning, heading to his father's. Another dead end. He'd been on the trip for forty-eight hours and had gained nothing. All of it was a grand gesture, like the flailing of some poor sucker falling off a cliff.

"You should stay with me," Marie said. "How are you going to get to the garage to pick up the RV otherwise?"

"No, thank you," Greg said. "I can call a taxi." The idea of sleeping in Marie's condo felt akin to lying down in a hole someone had just dug. He was going in circles now, back in the Buick with Marie. Another twenty-four hours before he could have the RV back. What would he do? Lie in bed, watching the hotel television. Gather meals from fast-food restaurants. Make a late-night barefoot pilgrimage to the hotel vending machine. He would do nothing; he would spend yet another twenty-four hours of his life doing nothing.

"If that's what you want," Marie said. "Let it be known that I tried to convince you otherwise." And then they were both quiet, Marie putting the Buick in cruise control, steadying the wheel with just one hand. Greg wanted to turn up the music, but he didn't feel allowed to, so it tittered on, low and distant, songs he thought he recognized but couldn't be sure. Soon he felt lulled by it all, the steady whir of the Buick, the blur of trees out the window, the inevitable nothingness that awaited him at the hotel. He closed his eyes. It felt like a miracle, the sleep that folded down over him, and he was grateful.

GJ came to visit them one summer in Birmingham. Marie needed a break was how she put it. *He's twenty-three years old, Greg. I don't know what else to do.* Greg suspected she was dating someone and that was really why she was shipping GJ off, but he couldn't justify feeling superior over that knowledge; he'd grabbed hold of Deb and left GJ with Marie and almost never looked back.

Every time he spoke to GJ on the phone, or when he'd come and stay in the Ramada downtown for a quick visit, taking GJ out for burgers and beers at the Hard Rock, GJ talked about his life like he had plans. He was going to sign up to be a cross-country truck driver. *I'll get to see Vegas, or the Grand Canyon, or Red Rocks.* But then he didn't show up for his drug test. Then GJ talked about becoming a plumber; a friend of his made *mad money* doing it, and the training was long but *not crazy hard, is what I heard.* Greg bought GJ the books he needed and the coverall uniform the technical school required. On a visit down to Orlando in the fall that year, GJ picked him up from the airport, and when he opened the trunk to toss Greg's suitcase in, Greg saw the books and the uniform still in their bags. *I'm going to start in the spring*, GJ said, squeezing Greg's shoulder like he needed consoling, and slammed the trunk. Then it was a job at a bookstore by the college, but that ended after six months because GJ didn't show up for work three separate times. Then it was back to the plumbing idea, maybe the air force, or maybe culinary school.

It excited GJ to talk about his plans. Saying them out loud made them real to him, Greg finally realized. And once they were real, there was no need to pursue them. It was good enough for GJ to simply have the idea. Then he could go back to his mother's condo and hide in his room, drinking when she was home, smoking when she wasn't. The first year of their marriage, he and Deb took a cruise, a knife-skills cooking class, spooned on the couch while watching evening television, and made love often. As the years went on Greg would say, *We oughta take that trip down to the Keys*, or *There's a new museum we should check out*, or *We should take photography lessons*. But they rarely did any of those things. Work was stressful, exhausting, both of them in the prime of their careers and racing to stay that way. Home was a refuge of silence, where there were no expectations and no pressures. So Greg could understand why it felt so good for GJ to lie to himself, lie to Greg and Marie, about his plans for the future, and then never find the wherewithal to follow through. It was the Greg part of GJ, the part Marie had once called *your depression issue*.

Another part of Greg wondered if it was partly Marie's fault, too; she was so controlling that she did everything for GJ when he was a child, even his homework, and he never learned to go it on his own. Or maybe GJ saw how adulthood was its own miasma of confusion and misery, Greg and Marie hating their jobs and each other, and their son decided it wasn't for him.

At nineteen GJ's car was found parked on a median in the middle of OBT. It was registered in Greg's name, so after it was towed they called him to come get it. GJ had taken the bus back to Marie's condo because he hadn't been able to find his car. Greg had done things that seemed on par when he was that age and drank a six-pack a night, so he had decided not to worry all that much about it. Even if it had taken place on OBT. Then at twenty-one GJ was pulled over on OBT and arrested for possession. The judge gave him a warning and one hundred hours of community service, which he'd completed with a drive Greg hadn't seen in years. It seemed to embarrass the boy, and it secretly thrilled Greg; he was hoping it truly was the bottom for GJ.

But only two years later there he was, fired at twenty-three from a car dealership, where he worked detailing new automobiles before their owners drove them off the lot. To Greg, it had seemed like the perfect job for the boy, a mindless kind of job that would exhaust his body and clear out his brain, help him go straight home and fall asleep instead of driving down OBT looking for his dealer.

"He showed up at work high," Marie said. "He fell asleep in a chair in the waiting room. Where the customers sit."

"How do you know all this?" Greg asked. He couldn't imagine GJ confessing any of it to Marie.

"Because I went down there to beg them for a second chance. But it wasn't the first time. It wasn't even the second time. It's your turn now, Greg. I need a break." She was going to St. Augustine for a week, she said, and she didn't feel comfortable leaving GJ in her condo all alone.

"It *is* our turn," Deb said in bed that night. She was lotioning her hands and the smell filled the room. *Plumeria*, the bottle said, whatever that meant.

GJ flew up on a Saturday. He had offered to drive himself up but Greg liked the idea that he wouldn't be able to bring drugs with him, what with bag inspections and security. They could drink together, at night on the small porch he and Deb had, could even sit in the new Jacuzzi with their ice-cold bottles if the evening was cool. It was a new thing he and Deb had been doing lately, sitting in the Jacuzzi with icy cocktails until they were almost asleep, then dragging themselves to bed and falling into darkness, a hard sleep that felt cleansing.

A woman at work had an addict daughter who was in rehab for heroin. *She can't drink when she gets out*, the woman had told Greg one night at happy hour. *She can't even* drink. They had cheersed solemnly.

Greg picked GJ up and they went for lunch at the Ale House. Then they went to the grocery store and Greg told him to toss whatever he liked to eat into the cart. He chose Fruity Pebbles, Pop Tarts, frozen pizzas, ice cream, lemonade. All the things Marie never allowed him to eat growing up. Greg added pasta sauce, whole-wheat noodles, a couple bagged salads that looked like they had shredded carrots in them. He and Deb weren't cooks; they often ate out or ate the leftovers from eating out the night before. Greg added a frozen vegetable lasagna and bags of frozen peas. At the last minute he wheeled over to Produce and pulled two bags of Fuji apples into the cart; he wanted GJ to see that there were other ways to eat, other ways to indulge. He also wanted GJ to report back to Marie that he was kind of a health freak, even as the scale was tipping over 220 pounds.

"Dad," GJ called. He was an aisle over; they couldn't see each other, but it touched Greg, this moment of his son calling to him, the way he did as a child when they were in a crowd.

"Yeah?" Greg called back.

"Check this out."

Greg wheeled the cart into the next aisle. GJ was pointing at a display featuring marshmallows, graham crackers, chocolate bars. "Remember when we went camping?"

"Hell, yeah," Greg said. "S'mores? Let's do it." GJ seemed a bit tired, a bit dazed, staring a little too long, but who didn't after an early-morning flight? He also seemed fundamentally himself, goofy and good-hearted. He had even gained weight; his arms looked tanned and muscular. He was only twenty-three, still basically a child. Still plenty of time.

GJ tossed the marshmallows, chocolate, and graham crackers into the cart. When they paid, Greg made sure GJ saw the total, which was more than a hundred and fifty dollars. He wanted the boy to know Greg was being extravagant, generous, doing all he could to make his son feel at home.

That night they cooked the pasta, the noodles so mushy that they fell apart in the sauce. The salad bowl with its mound of leaves and puddle of ranch sat untouched, Deb halfheartedly attempting to pass it around. Greg and GJ took turns getting each other beers, racing to refill Deb's wineglass, laughing and elbowing each other like they were both a lot younger. GJ handed Greg his lighter to get the grill going, and they used meat forks to roast the marshmallows over the blue flames.

The meat forks got white-hot, and GJ closed his lips over a mallow before Greg could warn him. "Ah, fuck," GJ hissed, throwing the fork on the ground, and Greg felt so tipsy, so *buzzed*, as he used to call it, that he drew his boy in and hugged him, slapping his back, rejoicing in hitting flesh and not bone.

"You two have fun," Deb said. "I'm going to bed."

It felt like too much work to get the Jacuzzi going; there was the switch you had to turn on, and then you had to adjust the temperature so it didn't boil you alive, and then you had to wait fifteen minutes, so he and GJ lay on the ground, in Deb's freshly mulched herb garden, leaning up on their elbows to sip from their fresh beers.

"Dad," GJ said.

"Hmm?" Greg asked. He was considering sleeping there, out in his yard under the night sky. It was chilly but convenient, and so soft.

"When you were my age, did you know you wanted to be an accountant?"

Greg thought. When he was twenty-three he was married to Marie, living in a garage their landlord claimed was a studio apartment. They had discussed divorce on their first wedding anniversary. He was out of college with a degree in finance, because *finance* sounded like *money*, which was what he needed more than anything. He had minored in history because he dreamed of becoming a teacher. On the day of his graduation, his mother had pulled him aside and said, *Now it's time for you to be a man and support your family. Teaching isn't going to do it.*

"No," Greg said. "But I knew I needed to be a man and support my family. Your mom and I, we knew we wanted kids. So I started doing secretarial work at a CPA firm, and everything fell into place after that." It was a half-honest answer. He wanted GJ to know that not knowing was okay, but that not knowing for the rest of his life was not okay.

GJ leaned up on his elbows and looked down at Greg. His lips were lined in chocolate. Greg ran his hand over his own mouth. "Did you ever worry that you don't want anything at all? Like, you don't want *anything*. You need air, food, whatever . . . But there's nothing you can honestly say you want."

"No," Greg said. He had always wanted. Money, sex, freedom, food. He wanted all of those things at various points in his life, so bad that his mouth watered.

"I know Mom sent me here because she's fed up with me."

"Yes," Greg said. It felt good, for a moment, to let Marie be the villain, but then he guiltily tried to soften the blow. "She loves you, but it's hard to watch someone you love go through hard times."

"I think this just might be who I am. The hard times, I mean. It's just me." He laughed. They were both sitting up now. The back of Greg's shirt was damp and the unseasonably cool air blew across it. He felt chilled to the bone.

"It won't be you forever," Greg said. He felt sure of it. All GJ needed was a purpose. Maybe he'd fall in love. Or maybe he'd stumble across a job he truly enjoyed. Everyone eventually found their way.

GJ laughed again. "Thanks," he whispered.

"You're going to be all right," Greg said. Something his own mother and father had never said to him.

"Yeah," GJ said. He upturned the bottle and pulled the dregs of his beer, his Adam's apple bobbing. He let out a loud guttural belch. Greg had taught him how to burp when he was a child, something that always made them laugh, and they laughed now, cheersing their empty bottles.

"Another?" Greg asked.

"Naw," GJ said. "I was thinking maybe I could go pick us up a DVD." Greg looked at him, the bloodshot eyes, the worn skin on his face as if he was ten years older. It was clear what he meant. He needed the car to drive around looking for a dealer.

"Now?" Greg asked.

"Yeah. We could have a double feature like we used to." They had done that only once, the way Greg remembered it. A night just before he and Marie separated, when they'd both felt exhausted enough to do something silly, like be together on a Saturday evening. They'd ordered pizza, watched a couple movies, and then Greg had carried GJ to bed. When he came back to the living room, Marie was lying on the couch, naked, her pajamas folded neatly next to her, the TV and the lights off and her skin a cold gray in the moonlight. *We can do this*, she said. *We just have to try harder.* He'd sunk into her; sometimes relief is disguised as exhaustion. He wanted to try harder, too. But in the morning, in the daylight, they were who they were again. Marie was clothed, drinking coffee, not meeting his eye; she was his soon-to-be ex-wife, not that beautiful alien who'd stroked his back and whispered, *See? See?* into his ear the night before. Had GJ noticed? Did he know they tried again but were too tired to try hard enough?

"There's a video store just ten minutes away," Greg said. "Can you be back in twenty-five minutes?"

"Of course," GJ said. "I already know the ones I'm going to get."

"Twenty-five minutes," Greg said again. "I'll wait for you."

GJ was gone four hours. Greg waited in one of the hard-backed dining chairs because it was by the window, but eventually he'd moved to the sofa in the living room, sitting in the darkness and falling asleep and waking when the light in the kitchen came on, GJ drinking water from the tap, slurping like a dog. Greg thought of standing up, signaling to GJ that he was there, watching him, but he didn't. He lay completely still, listening to his son drink water like he'd been wandering in a desert somewhere. Besides, he knew what the boy would say. *Sorry, Dad, I got lost.*

At the end of the week he, Deb, and Marie drove GJ up to rehab. At the end of thirty days he went home to Marie's, got a job as a valet at a steakhouse. He made it a year before his next rehab. He made it another three years. He made it only six months after that. It felt like GJ held Greg by his ankles over a ravine. At any moment he could let go and the whole world would go tumbling past. Soon Greg stopped trying to right himself; he got used to everything being upside down. All the blood rushed to his numb head. Everything numb, eyes closed against the floor of the sky. And then nearly three years after that, it was GJ who fell off the face of the earth.

Greg realized he'd left his wallet in the RV only when he was standing at the front desk at the Homewood Suites, and only then after the woman in the cheap maroon vest asked him if she could see a credit card and a driver's license.

"Shit," he said.

"Sir," the woman said.

He walked to the lobby area, where there were old-fashioned phone booths with worn chairs the same color as the woman's vest. He found the crumpled paper the tow truck driver had given him and called the number listed there. They were closed Sundays, the recording said. Greg laughed to himself. He had no wallet and no transportation. The woman in the maroon vest was openly staring at him.

Greg walked back to the desk. Pam, her name tag said. Manager in Training. Another Pam. Was there no Pamela left in this world?

"Pam," he said. "Would you be able to take a credit card over the phone? My wife can give you the numbers if we call her."

"I'm sorry, but that's not an option," she said, as if she were standing up to the school bully. Her hair was pulled back tightly into a ponytail of wet curls, her eyes upturned at the corners like she'd tortured her head into neatness.

He had been looking forward to a real shower; everything on his body felt filmed with oil or soap. He didn't have to look to see that there were lunules of sweat under each armpit and crude wet smiley faces under each pectoral. Occasionally he got a whiff of Italian dressing, which he knew was the way his undercarriage smelled after he hadn't bathed properly. He wanted to explain to Pam that he was doing everyone a favor, trying to check in to this hotel. He wanted to tell her there were 47 tiles that he could see; he wanted to ask if he could go behind the desk and count the ones he couldn't. He wanted to ask her if she knew 47 was a prime number, ask if she also found it odd 49 wasn't a prime number. Instead he thanked her and walked out, through the rotating door and out onto the thin sun-bleached walkway. Cars were zooming past, racing down I-Drive to work or church or the grocery store or back home from Grammy's or down to OBT to do whatever. It was a tourist's purgatory, I-Drive, restaurants and hotels and T-shirt shops, Ripley's Believe It or Not and a ferris wheel and four lanes of road that carried you a short jaunt to and from the theme parks. Greg thought he could hear screams on the wind, a roller coaster apexing and then shooting straight down. He dialed Marie from a pay phone outside a Denny's, and ten minutes later he was in the Buick, joining the caravan of humans passing each other in purgatory.

"Thank you," Greg said. "And I'm sorry. To be putting you out like this."

She shrugged. "I was the one who invited you to stay in the

first place." The sun was the color of a mango, slipping down the horizon and dragging all the blue with it. The strawberry air freshener was swinging from the rearview mirror again. Greg felt grateful for it, happy to smell something other than his own body.

Marie's condo had a large walk-in shower with two nozzles, one aimed at his midsection and one dumping rainwater on his head. She had a loofah and body wash with "exfoliating micro-beads." She had a seemingly endless supply of hot water. He washed himself, and then he sat on the cool tile floor, and then he lay on it, using the loofah as a cushion for the back of his head. The gentle patter of rain on his crotch was a revelation, subtly pleasureful but not enough to cause any real kind of excitement. He once had to spend a month sleeping flat on his back on the floor by his bed after he'd pulled something reaching for a shot glass. He hadn't been able to lie on his back in quite some time. He was afraid he wouldn't be able to get back up, pinned under his own weight. And it was true, it was difficult to rise, but when the water finally cooled, he found that all he had to do was fling his weight to the side and use his elbow to push up. His heart was pounding and he felt like a walrus trying to mount a bicycle, but it was possible; he'd done it.

His clothes weren't wadded on the floor where he'd left them. In their place were a pair of men's sweatpants and a T-shirt that looked like it would fit but be snug. They were GJ's, Greg realized. Just old crap he'd left behind, but they felt precious to Greg, and he felt grateful to Marie for offering them. When had she come in to exchange the clothing, though? Had she seen him flat on his back, eyes closed and mouth open slightly, enjoying the water falling on his balls? He decided not to consider it for too long. He had GJ's clothes; that was what to focus on.

She was in the kitchen, holding a fat wineglass, watching the microwave.

"I'm heating up Chinese," she said. "If you want some."

It felt like he hadn't eaten since the bag of tacos; the Chinese smelled salty and unctuous and his mouth flooded with saliva. "That'd be great," he said.

"Wine?"

"Does the pope shit in the woods?"

"Ha."

He wondered if he should go into the kitchen and get himself a glass, but the kitchen was short and narrow, really only room for one normal-sized person or two smaller people. Definitely not room for him to push in, pin her against the counter with the fleshy dome of his heavy belly just so he could pour a glass of wine. And it was her kitchen, not his. He was a guest.

"I'm sorry I took so long," he said. "It's been a long day." She handed him a glass. The wine was ice cold and so tart that it seemed to fizz. She had always preferred this kind of wine, wine that tasted and smelled like urine to Greg, but now he just felt thankful for every icy swallow.

"For me, too," Marie said. The microwave beeped. She took out a container and stuck her finger deep into the middle of it. "Needs a little more time."

He held his empty glass up. "Guess I'm thirsty," he said. He was often guilty of trying to explain away his appetite, to justify his rages of hunger. At parties with Deb he would tell others in line at the buffets that he was getting plates for him and his wife, when really he was filling two plates just for him. At restaurants he sometimes claimed he hadn't eaten all day, when in reality he'd probably been eating all day. At the bar he'd say it had been a long day, or he was thirsty, or he'd drink two at one bar and go to the next bar and drink three. They fell out of his mouth, these excuses, these lies, as if they were stones he'd been holding in his cheeks for too long. He knew it was better to say nothing at all, to stop calling attention to himself, but the stones still fell, *plop plop plop*. Marie upended the bottle over his glass; it grew heavy in Greg's hands and he felt a bit more relaxed. He wanted to ask her to fill another glass up, just so he could always have one on deck, but he couldn't even bring himself to ask Deb to do it. It was strictly a ritual he performed alone, on nights when Deb had a class or an event or book club.

"Why was it a long day for you?" Greg asked. He was careful to strip anything that might be mistaken for scorn out of his voice.

"Well, after you left, I sat here and cried," she said.

"I'm sorry," he said.

"No," she said. "It was good. I had a lot to flush out." Marie talked about her issues as if they were things she could purge, flush, work out, strip away. But she was not a crier, or at least she wasn't in the years they'd been married, so Greg did feel guilty, even as he felt a bit superior, like he'd won something.

"I felt bad," she said. "No. I *feel* bad. Do you remember when we got divorced? Didn't you think we'd be done with each other by now?" She waited, watching Greg, the microwave heating the acrid food behind her. He nodded. "And yet here we are. It's been so many years. It's been so long. But we can't be rid of each other."

"GJ needs us," Greg said. He took another rancid swallow. "That's why we're here right now."

"It just feels like time moved on and we couldn't keep up." She took a long pull of wine, gulping like it was water. "When I'm around you, I feel like the past twenty years were a dream I had while I was stuck in quicksand."

"Okay, Marie," Greg said.

"No, I'm sorry. I don't want us to fight. I just want to be honest with you. I just want to hear if it's the same for you. If you also feel stuck. Isn't this surreal for you at all?" she asked. She opened the fridge and pulled out another bottle of wine.

"It is," Greg said. "But, honestly, my main focus is on GJ. Here, let me," he said, gesturing to the wine opener. She handed the bottle and the gadget over to him, walked around the kitchen bar to stand next to him with her empty glass.

"We're old," she said. "You've been married to Deb almost as long as you were married to me." She held out her glass.

"Marriage is never easy," he said. He poured until the glass was nearly full, and then he topped his own glass off. He didn't know why he was talking about marriage with Marie; he didn't know why he felt compelled to give her any kind of a glimpse into the dry-wall of a relationship he and Deb had.

"Do you ever wonder why we chose each other?" she asked. The microwave beeped, but she made no move to check on the food. She was a bit drunk, Greg realized. Her hair was frizzed at the roots and her face sagged.

"What do you mean?" He took a step back.

"We were both virgins," she said. "You were this gangly"—she flapped her hand—"hungover kid, and I was going to go to New York and be an artist. Instead we hoofed it to the dorm and couldn't get our clothes off fast enough. I hated you at first sight. Did you know that? You looked like you came from a Dumpster. Why did we choose each other? Why did we choose this life?"

He had loved her at first sight. The girl of his dreams, the dreams he had deep inside his own subconscious, dreams he would never remember, the kind of dreams that produce déjà vu and doppelgangers and surprise pregnancies and make momentary soul mates out of strangers.

"We were kids," he said. "We were almost ten years younger

than GJ is now." She shook her head. "We were horny," he said. "Okay? We were horny and maybe that's just the long and short of it." He drank his glass of wine in slurping gulps, poured himself another. His head felt coated in a light fuzz, as if he were a dandelion. It wasn't enough; he felt afraid that Marie didn't have nearly enough to drink in the condo.

Marie was laughing. "That's it," she said. "That's exactly it. We were just horny!" The microwave beeped again, a shrill reminder. "*Horny* is such an old-person way to say it." She looked at him, and Greg had the feeling that she was going to ask him something he didn't know how to answer.

"I'm horny," she said, like she was trying it on. She stepped forward, filling the space he'd tried to create between them, and then she slammed her wineglass down onto the Formica bar, and then she pulled him by the ears toward her and mashed her mouth onto his. It felt like grappling, her pulling his arms around her, Greg trying to maneuver away from the bar and all the glass, the bar stools scraping against the tile in loud honks, the assault happening in his mouth with her tongue fishing around and the realization that it wasn't entirely unpleasant. They had kissed tentatively that day in her dorm room, but it made sense, after everything, with their son missing or dead and never fully theirs to begin with, that now they'd be gnawing, gulping, consuming each other. They'd traded one extreme for another. Gentleness for meaning it. Greg was supporting almost her full weight; she was pulling him down by the ears again and his back was beginning to whine. He tried to lean on one of the bar stools, but it skidded away from him and he fell, clutching Marie, pulling her down with him.

"Wait," he tried to say. The fall had knocked the wind out of him. Marie sat up, holding her forehead, straddling the dome of his torso. She reached behind and dragged her hand across the front of his sweatpants until she found the halfhearted swelling, and then she yanked at his waistband until he lifted his hips despite himself, helping her get them down almost to his knees. "Wait," he said again. His heart felt like a foot trying to kick its way out of cement. "I need to sit up."

Marie dismounted and crouched next to him. She offered a hand and helped pull him into a seated position, his back against the wall. Greg's head felt swelled with blood, sweat pilling up on his forehead and cheeks. His throat felt raw and he couldn't catch his breath. Was this a heart attack? He'd read that the pain begins in the left arm, but his left arm felt the same as his right arm did.

"Shh," Marie was saying. "Count to ten." She took his hand and drew the numbers into his palm: 1, 2, 3 . . . . He preferred stopping at 9, which was the last solo integer. But he let her go to 10, because it felt good, and because his breathing was evening out. "I'll get you a glass of water," she said.

He heard her run the tap, drink a few gulps herself. When she returned she sat next to him and they passed the cup of water between them. It was a glass from their married days. He remembered keeping one just like it on his nightstand to sip from in the middle of the night, or to pass to Marie on the odd night that they'd both been drunk enough to want to fuck.

"What was that?" he asked.

Marie finished what was left of the water, then pushed the glass across the tile. It came to a stop by a woven magazine rack she kept near the couch. "I don't know," she said.

Greg's body felt tired, like he'd just jogged a mile. His ass pushed into the tile floor uncomfortably, the tile pushing right back just as hard. He shifted so he was facing Marie.

"It's like when you're young, time matters so much," she said. "We took so many pictures of GJ, do you remember? And then when you're old, you realize time only matters when you say it does. They're just pictures." She looked at him. She had a red smudge on her forehead; she must have smacked it when they went down. "It was just a divorce."

"I think I know what you mean," he said. He crawled over and retrieved the glass, then held it to Marie's forehead. Her face was the same face, just let down a little. She was still Marie, the Marie he'd loved and hated.

She took the glass from him. "I've been alone a long time, Greg."

"I know you have."

"It's hard to love someone you don't like. It takes everything out of you."

"He'll come back," Greg said. She nodded. They sat in the quiet for a while. The microwave beeped every ninety seconds. He closed his eyes and counted. His ass felt numb, which was just as well. He heard Marie shift, and then he felt her hand on his. He kept his eyes closed while she shifted again, moving over him. This time there was no kissing, just breath in each other's ears, the soft rustling as she removed her pants and then his jockeys, Marie murmuring, "I have to wet you first," her mouth on him but just for two brief swipes, and then the plunge in. Still a shock, that plunge. Still a miracle, that wet grasping warmth, especially now, when it felt like his whole body was numb and had been for decades. It was a marvel, how you learned to do something with someone and you never forgot it. It felt like he and Marie were helping each other through a necessary procedure, like getting gas or a root canal. They had made GJ and they were a family and this was a familiar thing, this pushing and pulling, this working together. She still made the same noises, still that series of gasps near the end. She still knew how to bear down, grip him at the base with her vagina, and let them pulse together. How did she learn how to do that? Deb often stopped moving, stock still, receiving him the way a statue receives the chisel. His mouth flapped open; he leaned his head back, breathing hard, pulling in strands of her hair and then blowing them back out on the exhale. Marie stood and went into the kitchen, coming back with two red-and-white-striped dish towels. She handed one to him and began dabbing at herself, openly, nothing to hide. Greg did the same, wiping and folding and wiping and folding until the towel was the size of a hoagie.

Marie pulled her pants on and slid down the wall beside him. "Tell Deb that now we're even." She had always assumed that he and Deb had had an affair toward the end of their marriage. But it hadn't been Deb; it had been another woman, what was her name? Blond curly hair. On his knees before her. Hand job at the drive-thru. He had been drunk nearly every day back then and these were the only things he remembered of her, foul keepsakes he rarely drew upon. He'd let Marie think it was Deb so she wouldn't have to wonder if there were others. Not to protect her, but to protect himself.

"I'm sorry," he said.

"Don't be," she said. "It's what I wanted."

He did his best to shimmy his pants back on, but without standing up he could only get them to web across his crotch. The doorbell rang, two short notes like a child's piano. Marie looked at him like he'd invited someone over and hadn't told her. Whoever it was began to knock, first in friendly raps and then more urgently, as if the person had turned his or her fist and begun to really wail on the door.

"GJ," Greg said. It flew out of his mouth before he had the chance to truly consider it. But who else could it be? He pushed himself onto his knees but Marie was faster. She tried to run for the door but tripped over the glass and fell, crawling through the shards as fast as she could.

"Wait," Greg said. Now he was on his feet, too. Marie's knee was leaving wet red stamps across the tile. "You're bleeding, just hold on!" He tiptoed over the glass, pulling his pants up the rest of the way, trying to avoid slipping in the crimson smudges. Marie pulled herself up using the door handle, undid the two dead bolts, and swung the door open. A short Asian woman in a ballcap stood there, holding a pizza box.

"Oh, fuck you," Marie said. She let the door swing shut in the woman's face. She turned and walked past Greg, down the hall into the bathroom. "Fucking tile floors," she yelled. He heard the water running. He found a broom in the small closet by the kitchen and swept up what glass he could see, used the dish towel he'd cleaned himself with to wipe up the blood. When he was finished he could still hear the water running. He crept down the hall, not sure if he should intrude. He remembered the bathroom they shared at the second house they lived in, back when GJ was only about five or six, how the toilet and shower were behind a door, how it felt like he'd never take a shit alone again, how privacy became one of the commodities they bartered back and forth, his in the morning and hers at night. He'd often fall asleep before she'd leave what they came to call the water closet, and eventually he realized she was doing that on purpose.

Marie was sitting on the bathroom counter with her feet in the small bowl sink, holding a washcloth to her knee, letting the water run down her ankles and into the drain. Greg turned it off and sat across from her.

"I'll take you to the garage first thing," Marie said. "To pick up the RV. And then I'll go file a missing persons report."

"Thank you." The box of bandages was still on the counter. Greg took one out and unwrapped it. Marie moved the washcloth and he could see a small cut, its little sliver of blood. He pressed the bandage to it.

"I really thought it was him for a second," she said.

"Me, too." It had seemed to make sense, in that moment, things finally clicking into place; GJ showing up at his mother's house because it was really the only home he had. Lured there, maybe, by the psychic pull of his parents together in the same place, the vibrations of worry. But what made even more sense, what was even more likely, Greg realized, was that a stranger would show up at the wrong unit with a pizza.

"I guess it's good he didn't see us like this," Marie said, folding the bloody washcloth.

"Right." Greg wondered if GJ was also sending psychic vibrations to him and Marie, if he was somewhere concentrating very hard on getting his parents to hear him, if it was pulsing out of his subconscious like squiggly green fumes in a child's drawing of a trash can. Would he truly drive home tomorrow? After only three days? He couldn't decide if it was more pathetic to do that or to keep driving aimlessly around Florida, coast to coast, sweating years off his life. But he also couldn't decide if he was ready to drive home, wait for Deb in the parking lot of the rental place, lean in and kiss her cheek through the window, pretend nothing had happened. He had become an expert at doing that toward the end with Marie. She was right; time mattered only if you believed it did.

But in a sense nothing *had* happened. He'd had sex with Marie, who was once his wife, who was the mother of his missing and very sick son. Sex was a survival mechanism that led to the survival of a species. He and Marie were Parents of the Lost, a species all their own. They had reached for each other and done what had to be done to keep surviving. In the mirror above the sink he could see both of their faces. The him that wasn't looking into a mirror felt forty-one. And he knew Marie felt forty-two. In the mirror they leaped forward nearly twenty years. Half of his ass was hanging off the counter. His belly felt as large as his wingspan. The acne on his neck was red and irritated. Marie had mounted *that*? He felt grateful to her, and sorry for her.

She blotted her feet with a hand towel. "I'm going to bed, I think," she said. "The sheets are folded on top of the dresser in the guest room."

Greg nodded and thanked her, but then he followed behind her into her room and into her bed, and they lay on their sides face-to-face, the way they had when GJ was an infant and every noise he made was a bullhorn of terror in their hearts, and they slept until the sun made a dull yellow line in the thin space where her curtains met.

The shitty blue truck. The shitty brown car. A slightly less shitty red car. Kisses with tongue, then kisses with no tongue, then no kisses. A silver convertible. Kmart photo shoots, comb marks in his and GJ's hair. Fabric ties, silk ties. Their beer phase. Neighbors, friends. Inside jokes. Their wine phase. Innuendo, endless innuendo. Working late, working weekends, "working." Cocktail phase. Road trips, car games, buckets of ice in the motel hallway. Their highball, straight-up phase. Dad, can I have a sip? Sure. Mom, can I try? Sure. Picnics, evening television, yelling. The blinking VCR clock. Eight o'clock. EIGHT OH ONE! Sex, mean sex. Lingerie for Christmas, the wrong kind. Shoulders and neck stiffening to cement. Can you? Can you just? Jesus Christ. I'm trying as hard as I can. Nine o'clock, ten o'clock, blink, blink, blink. Dad? Mom? Mom, where's Dad? Dad, is Mom okay? Shut up, kid.

The last time Greg saw GJ it had been at Christmas. This was the thing he couldn't bring himself to face. He'd come down on his own; Deb had decided to fly to California to visit her sister for the holiday. Greg rented his usual room at the Ramada and waited for GJ at the hotel bar on Christmas Eve. Lately he and Marie had forgone gifts or money as presents, since GJ tended to sell whatever he was given or spend the money on drugs, but on that day Greg had a present, a new leather wallet with GJ's initials and a crisp fifty-dollar bill inside it. It was Christmas, and he wanted to give his son something, and he was tired of worrying what might happen.

GJ was late, but he was always late, plenty of time for Greg to steady himself on another Maker's. It was raining outside, as close to a white Christmas as Orlando ever came. When GJ finally walked in his hair and shoulders were wet, and he whipped his hair back and forth like a dog. He was wearing an old button-down shirt of Greg's, purple and green vertical stripes, tucked into a pair of relatively clean jeans. He had put on weight, which made Greg smile, because it meant he wasn't using. He'd been out of rehab for four months; maybe it had taken.

"Hey, Dad," GJ said, closing his thick hand over Greg's. Greg pulled him in for a hug, GJ's hair wet on his cheek.

"You hungry?" Greg asked.

"A little," GJ said. "But hey, is that the Volvo parked right out front?" GJ asked. Greg had been trying to pull him toward the bar, envisioning finishing his drink while GJ ate the peanuts and popcorn, and then settling up and walking to dinner, rain or no, at the sushi place two blocks away. But GJ didn't budge.

"Yeah," Greg said.

"You can't park on this side of the street anymore," GJ said. "Only cops and city vehicles can, now that the mayor's office is just next door."

It felt surreal, talking to GJ about something as banal as parking. That GJ knew there was a mayor, much less where his office was, made Greg feel like laughing, hugging his son all over again. Even better: it felt like GJ was trying to brag to Greg, to show him that he had changed.

"Guess I better move it, then," Greg said.

"No," GJ said. "You've been drinking." He nodded his head over Greg's shoulder, at his two empty glasses. Rehab could sometimes make GJ a teetotaler, right up until he fell off the wagon himself. "I can move it." He held his hand out for the keys.

GJ's eyes were clear, the pupils a normal size. He smelled clean; not even a trace of cigarette smoke. Four months out of rehab and showing up in a nice shirt. Greg pulled the keys out of his pocket and dangled them in front of GJ.

"You can park it in the Ramada garage," he said. "They'll just charge the arm and the leg to my room."

GJ grinned. "Order me a Coke," he said. Greg watched him jog back the way he came, holding the door for a woman running in with a newspaper over her head and then ducking back outside himself. The woman settled at the bar, using the small cocktail napkins to dab the rain from her arms. Greg felt so happy, so hopeful, with the delicate warmth running through his body from the Maker's and the night he was about to have with his son. He told the bartender to get the woman a drink, whatever she wanted, on him, but the woman shook her head, said she was waiting on a friend.

After twenty minutes Greg walked through the gold doors, down the short hallway, and out into the parking garage. There were inkblots of oil, the smell of air freshener and exhaust. Plenty of empty spaces. He walked over to the attendant and asked if a Volvo had come through.

"Nothing in the past hour," the attendant said, flapping her newspaper.

Greg went back to the bar to wait. Another Maker's and then back out into the garage. The attendant shook her head when she saw him coming. The bartender hadn't seen his son come back in. GJ wasn't answering his phone and neither was Marie. Greg thought about calling the police, reporting his car stolen, but it was Christmas. Instead he took out the fifty from the wallet and paid the bartender for his drinks, walked away without his change.

In the morning Greg saw plenty of cars parked along the mayor's side of the street. At the corner he saw the Volvo, its right front tire at an angle, the whole car at a diagonal. GJ was asleep in the passenger seat, his mouth open and his eyebrows furrowed as if he were in the middle of yelling. Greg tried the driver's door and it was unlocked. He got in and slammed the door, but GJ didn't stir. It smelled like booze and vomit but Greg couldn't see where it was coming from. The striped shirt from the night before was in a wet wad in the backseat; a parking ticket was stuck to the window. Greg honked the horn and GJ twitched, his arms flopping open. He looked around, like he had no idea where he was, and when his eyes fell on Greg he began to cry.

"I'm sorry, Dad," GJ said. He was crying so hard that he wailed into his hands, like he was trying to catch the sounds. "I'm sick," he said. "I've been doing things." He doubled over, wailing louder now. The seatback behind him had a large splash of something white on it, likely the vomit, Greg realized. "I do things for money. I don't even know why I need it so bad. Last night I let a guy—" He started heaving, and Greg reached across him to open the door. GJ turned and vomited onto the sidewalk. Greg could hear church bells ringing out, Christmas morning, a child is born. GJ had once told him his car had been stolen, that it was parked in the driveway of a guy he knew but he couldn't remember where the guy lived. Greg called the cops and they tracked the car down to the home of a man that said GJ had sold it to him for five hundred dollars and two six-packs. Another time, GJ said he'd been forced to sell drugs for a man who held his girlfriend hostage, so he'd done it, and that's how he'd gotten arrested. The lies came to GJ as easy as air.

"Hey," Greg said, in as calm and soothing a voice as he could muster. "Hey, son."

GJ pulled himself back into the car, his face red and puffy and slimed with tears and snot. He hadn't cried this hard in years, not since he was a child and things mattered to him. But Greg couldn't bring himself to believe him.

"I'm done," Greg said. He reached into the backseat and grabbed the shirt, holding it out to GJ. "I want you out of the car."

GJ took the shirt, looking from it to Greg like he wasn't sure what either were. "I—I need help, Dad," GJ said.

"I know you do," Greg said. He began lightly pushing GJ on the arm, nudging him to get up and out. "And I hope you find it." It was something one of the television addiction counselors said. *I hope you find help. Without me*, it implied. You're on your own; we're all on our own. His own mother had changed the locks as soon as he went away to college, disposed of him as easily as the quarter-inch of ash at the end of her cigarette that she tapped into a dish. He suddenly felt a perverse, angry gratitude to her for that kind of a push; it had gotten him out of that house for good. Greg pushed against his son harder, GJ not so much pushing back as hunkering down, determined to stay in the car. Tough love, self-preservation, both of them hanging off a cliff; who would Greg save? He felt a surge of rage course from his trunk into his arms. *Fuck you*, he screamed inside his head at his sweaty, sick son. *Fuck you for being weak.*

"Stop it," GJ said. Greg pushed even harder, using both hands now. He lunged with all the strength he had, bracing one foot against the driver's door.

"Out," Greg said. "Get the hell out of my car."

GJ landed on his hands and knees. Greg pulled the door closed, locking it quickly, and maneuvered the Volvo out into the slow line of traffic. He did not let himself look in the rearview mirror. When he got back to his room, the car parked in the parking garage in as hidden a spot as he could find, he threw the leather wallet into the trash and covered it with wads of toilet paper. He ordered room service, a wilted spinach salad and a bottle of red, and then he drove home in the afternoon.

When Greg was back in West Virginia, GJ tried calling, and then e-mailing him. One e-mail simply read, *Sorry.* The next one read, *Fuck you, you don't get to abandon me.* The final e-mail read, *I hope one day you'll forgive me.* And then Marie called asking if he knew where GJ was.

The road was emptier now that it was Monday; cars snugly parked in corporate spaces or in the lots behind the stores or restaurants or wedged inside parking garages rather than rushing down the highway on their way home or to the theme parks or, like Greg, heading out on a road trip. He'd paid five hundred dollars to have all four tires replaced, and when they mentioned that the oil was low he paid for that, too, plus a new air-conditioning filter, and a small fee for filling up the water tank and replacing the shitty showerhead nozzle. He felt like he owed it to the RV, and it was good to focus on problems that could be solved. He ran the list over and over in his head as he sat in the frigid waiting room, watching oil-smudged mechanics work over the RV and a two-door Honda through the windows to the garage. Tires, oil, filter, water, showerhead. Tires, oil, filter . . . After he woke up in Marie's bed, he found her dressed and drinking a glass of orange juice in the kitchen. He knew she probably ran the tap into it for three seconds; it had always been a habit of hers to water juice down.

"I'll take you as soon as you're dressed," she said. "I put your clothes on the toilet in the bathroom."

He wanted to answer her but his mouth felt dry. He smacked his lips, trying to gather enough saliva to loosen the rock of his tongue. He nodded and retraced his steps, down the hallway to the bathroom. He had showered the evening before, but parts of him felt sticky, and his hair was shooting up around his head like the plates of a stegosaurus. He had woken up alarmed, like he'd forgotten something, and standing in front of her, he'd still felt like there was something. What he'd wanted to say to her was something along the lines of *I'm sorry*. But it was clear Marie was going to pretend like it never happened, and then he'd wanted to say *Thank you*. Even so, he didn't feel like he was allowed another shower, so he splashed water on his hair and face and stuck a wet soapy hand down the front of his sweatpants. He and Marie had walked down the dark hallway together, into the brightness of the morning, Greg feeling seared by the sun, exposed the way a flayed body might feel exposed. They rode in silence to the garage, down Kirkman with its four lanes laced on either side with strip malls and churches and run-down or abandoned gas stations, up Colonial, which was more of the same, and down Bumby, which felt alternately like the old South and like tourists had lost their way and set up shop in the peeling and useless businesses on its corners. Marie pulled into the parking lot of the garage and left the engine running.

"Nice to see you," Greg said. He'd run through what to say and had come to that, a meaningless, ill-timed turd. Marie nodded, bless her for that, Greg thought. He leaned across the seat and hugged her as best as the car and their bodies would allow, one arm bracing himself against the seat and the other around her shoulders, his ear grazing her cheek. He felt a flurry of taps on his back, the kind of pat that was Deb's specialty, and it produced a warm shame in his middle that made him jerk away from Marie.

"Safe drive," Marie said.

"Thank you," Greg said. It was like they were performing that day on the library steps in reverse, when the heat had drawn them closer and closer together until they'd joined. Now they were peeling apart, dividing, something he was sure they'd done for good years ago. Maybe that meant GJ truly was dead; maybe their family was just ashes in a dish now. Greg got out of the car.

"Tell him to call me," Marie said, and drove away. She had been the one to ask him to leave, all those years ago. Mid-morning on a Sunday, sitting on their bed. *It's time for you to go*, she'd said. Calmly, her hands folded, his packed suitcase waiting by the door. It was one of the rare days in Florida where the sun felt friendly, like it was just playing at heat. Sky the blue of wiper fluid. Greg had taken his suitcase and driven straight to the rental office of an apartment complex he'd been eyeing. Marie had been the catalyst, because she knew it would never be him, because she knew he'd need a villain if he was going to go. And he had hated her for it, for being so sure, and for knowing him so well.

His wallet was still in the glove compartment. He paid the attendant, plugged his phone into the car charger, and pulled the RV out of the garage, into the parking lot, out onto Bumby, and onto the highway heading home.

He stopped at a KFC/Pizza Hut about thirty miles in and got a sweet tea, four biscuits, and two personal-sized cheese pizzas. He'd save two biscuits and one of the pizzas for later, he told himself, but he ended up rolling the second pizza into a burrito and eating it in three bites. He was starving; he longed for the Chinese takeout Marie had offered, could taste it on his tongue. His earliest memory: *Greg is becoming chubby.* His mother to his father, the way his father peered at him, examined him. His mother treated meals like an afterthought, something that was never a given. Greg often felt desperate for food back then. "Fuck you, Mother," he said now, but she had been dead and gone since GJ was a child, buried in her cream linen suit with the carton of Newports her sister had placed in her delicately crossed hands like a rosary, or a silk flower bouquet. His mother would have hated the idea.

The tacos he left at his father's were probably leaking in the bottom of the plastic mauve trash can the old man kept under the kitchen sink, the one his mother used to have in the guest bathroom. Who emptied the trash in a place like that? Was there a service, or did his father have to gather up the powdered bag, cinch it with his knobby arthritic fingers, and leave it on the curb? Greg wasn't sure which he hoped for more. But maybe Lydia took out the trash for him; maybe there were concessions the youngers made for the olders in retirement communities. Would he end up somewhere like that, with Deb? Where would Marie go? They'd only had one child and GJ was in no shape to make those kinds of decisions for them.

Deb. He hadn't called her in over twenty-four hours. He dialed home but there was no answer, and he didn't feel like leaving a message. He called her cell next; still no answer. She'd see that he'd called, and that would probably be enough. He was approaching the turnoff for 95, which he'd take up the right side of Florida for two hundred miles or so. There was a sign for Weeki Wachee, a tourist attraction on the left side of Florida where women wore glimmering fish tails and long thick wigs and clamshell bras and whirled slowly underwater, their large eyes staring out as if what they saw wasn't just one big blur. They'd gone there, once, as a family. He, Marie, and GJ. GJ had read about it in the pink paperback travel guide on Florida Greg had purchased back before they moved there.

"Real mermaids," GJ had said, holding the book up so Greg could see. A black-and-white photo showed a woman in a cheap costume, touching the tip of her tail with one graceful hand and waving with the other. A smaller image was in color and looked like it was from the '50s. It showed two mermaids perched on a large rock, one bright green tail and one bright blue one, the women's candy-pink lips, and the blur of a crowd behind them. GJ was eleven years old, too old in Greg's estimation to believe that mermaids were real, but it seemed like an opportunity was being handed to him, the opportunity to dazzle his son, the opportunity to act like a family, to do something normal. He and Marie had been talking about divorce; it loomed over their house like a black cloud bowing with rain.

They drove over on a Saturday, stopping for Cokes on the way. They passed the Rachel's and Gentleman's Choice and Booby Trap strip clubs that Greg attended in descending order of sobriety. And here he was in the daylight, taking his son to see half-naked women dance.

It was just a crappy, run-down tourist trap. Flaking stucco, patchy grass, walkways that needed repaving. Every forty-five seconds or so the women had to suck air from a long tube, like it was a hookah party under there, and Greg found himself holding his breath along with them. It was stressful, and Marie was barely paying attention, staring off and fidgeting, but GJ seemed riveted. He held his elbows in his hands and stared into the giant fish tank in the slackmouthed way he did when he watched television. Greg tried to see what he saw. The women in the tank didn't wear wigs, their hair moving around as slow as a dream; their breasts were disappointingly small and some of them had loose flesh at their waists. Greg leaned over to whisper in GJ's ear. "You like it, buddy?" GJ nodded. Finally it was time for the mermaids to have their break, so the thin crowd had to file out of the viewing area and mill around or leave.

"I'm ready to go," GJ said.

"You are?" Greg asked. He had expected to have to come up with a long explanation about why they had to go; it was a longish drive back and he wanted to be home before sunset so he could cut the grass (but really so he had time to shower and change before heading out for the night); he was even prepared to promise that they could stop for McDonald's.

"Yeah."

GJ and Marie were already walking to the car, and Greg jogged a bit to catch up with them. On the way home, they both fell asleep, Marie's head against the window and GJ's bobbing against his chest. The roadside fled by in a conveyor of green. Greg was thirsty, but not for the sweating Coke in his cup holder, and not for the half bottle of water in Marie's purse. He guessed he wouldn't get a real drink until about eight o'clock that night, but that was fine, it was something to look forward to.

"Dad." GJ was awake now, staring at Greg in the rearview mirror.

"Yeah," Greg said.

"I don't think Mom liked it there," GJ said.

"What makes you say that?"

"I could just tell."

"Hmm." GJ was developing a habit of speaking for Marie; he'd told Greg at the grocery store the previous week that she was having trouble eating dairy. He worried over his mother, checking and rechecking and reporting back. "Well, we went there so you could see it," Greg said. "I'm sure she was happy to be there because you were happy to be there."

"She likes the library," GJ said. "And she likes that garden place. Maybe next weekend we can do that instead."

"Okay," Greg said. He could feel that thing at the back of his throat, that thing that made him want to snap at GJ, but again he swallowed it down. Did GJ worry over *him* this way?

"Do you think some of those ladies had started new lives?" GJ asked.

"What?" Greg asked. He was still trying to swallow the lump down, still trying not to point out to GJ that Marie could fend for herself, that she was actually a cold bitch who was threatening to take all his money and the house.

"The mermaids," GJ said. "Did it seem like some of them had come there to become someone else?"

The car was slowing, Greg realized. He'd taken his foot off the gas, trying to keep up with the wild swings of what GJ was saying. He pushed down on the pedal to try to even his speed with the traffic around him.

"I guess it's possible," he said. He didn't know how to answer; he wasn't sure what GJ was getting at. "Why are you thinking about something like that?"

"I don't know," GJ said. He began playing with the electronic window controls, his window softly whirring up and then down. "It's just something I think about sometimes."

"Your mother's not moving to Weeki Wachee to become a mermaid," Greg said, trying to force a laugh into his voice. He watched GJ nod to himself.

"Oh, I know that," GJ finally said, his window whirring up.

"He was talking about *you*," Marie said that night, watching him getting dressed. Her arms were crossed; she had that tone in her voice. In eight months he'd be bringing that suitcase to the car, driving to the apartment to slide his credit card across the table for the security deposit. "He thinks *you're* going to start a whole new life."

But now Greg wasn't sure who or what GJ had been talking about. Was it a clue, this billboard rushing toward him, getting larger and larger? Should he take the exit that would take him west, toward Weeki Wachee? Did he believe that GJ fled there? To what? Sweep up those dingy walkways; help the women in and out of their tails; force bravado into his voice as he announced each set? Start a whole new life?

No. He didn't believe that. He drove past the exit that would take him to the mermaids; he pushed down on the gas so he could get to I-95 as quickly as possible.

And then he saw the kid again, up ahead, knee-deep in the wild grass growing in the median. Same idiotic beanie, same backpack, same slouch, pointing his thumb north this time.

"Oh, for fuck's sake," Greg said, because this *did* feel like a sign.

Greg had to cut across three lanes of traffic to get on the median side, and there was no shoulder to pull onto. He put on his hazards and slowed, angling the RV into the grass so it was half in the road and half out. Cars honked and swerved around him and he rolled down the window to wave them off. The kid jogged backward as Greg advanced, like the RV was a bull Greg barely had control of. When he finally had it stopped he had to look back to see the kid, ambling around the rear bumper, watching his feet like the grass held snakes or jewels.

"Hey," Greg said when the kid was even with his window. "You remember me?"

The kid was thin, angular, like his body had been made using spare elbows. He smiled easily, revealing dark pink gums and a gap between his front teeth. GJ had a gap, too.

"Yeah, man," the kid said. "Sure do." Something winked from his ear: a square diamond stud that looked too heavy and too grandmotherly. Was this the same kid? Greg didn't remember the earring or the smile. But then, he'd been crying the last time they saw each other.

"Where you headed to now?" Greg asked.

"Cassadaga," the kid said. It was like it'd just come to him, this destination.

"Another concert?"

"Yeah," the kid said, smiling wider now. "Something like that."

Greg mostly wanted to roll the window back up and pull back out into traffic. The passenger seat was piled with wrappers and GJ's sweatpants. He wanted to get home and put it all behind him. He longed for his living room; he longed for boredom and a shower at hand. If only Deb weren't there. It felt like the minute she saw him everything that had happened with Marie would be laid bare, like it was playing on a television embedded in his gut. Or, worse, Deb wouldn't suspect a thing, and what he feared was true: it didn't matter; none of it mattered at all, and he would hold his secret inside him forever, branching out into his heart, his guts, his lungs.

His father had accused him of looking for GJ only in the most obvious places. This detour to Cassadaga was his chance to look somewhere else, and to hide by searching.

"Get in," Greg said. He flung the detritus from the passenger seat into the cavity behind him, and the kid pulled himself up and in.

He said his name was Benji. He was going to Cassadaga, "the psychic capital of the world," to converse with his mother or Kurt Cobain through the spiritual realm. He was going to find a job as a waiter or a dishwasher or something so he could afford to live for a while.

"I'm looking for my son," Greg said.

"Oh, yeah?"

Now Greg was even more sure that this wasn't the same kid; he seemed to have no memory of their previous meeting, only days ago.

"Where's he at?" Benji asked.

"I don't know. That's what I'm trying to find out."

"Well, someone in Cassadaga might be able to tell you. Even if he's not dead." He put a hand on Greg's arm. It was warm and dry and felt rough with dirt. "I've been practicing," the kid said. "It's all about honing your intuition. You work with what you have." He closed his eyes. "Like sharpening a piece of flint on a rock."

Greg gripped the steering wheel. The kid's hand felt heavy, anchoring his arm in place. Benji opened his eyes. "You know, like with an arrowhead." He waited for Greg to nod, and then he dropped his hand. His eyes were pale and blue, the color of water after a drop of turquoise paint has been added. Like the kid had stared directly into the sun for so long it had started to bleach all the life out. "I didn't see anything," he said. "But I'm getting a strong indication that your son is still alive. His name is GJ?"

Greg's stomach dropped. "Yes," he said. He didn't know if he should pull over again, give Benji his full attention, ask him how he knew that, what else he knew.

"Yeah, I remembered that from last time," he said, and Greg's stomach dropped again.

"I didn't think you . . . you remembered," Greg said.

"Of course!" Benji said. "But yeah, I rooted around asking about GJ and I didn't get anything, but that means I also didn't get that weird gong sound that happens when I find out someone is dead. Here." He put his hand on Greg's arm again. "Yeah, no, still nothing. But the good news is *something* brought us together. And it was probably your son. Maybe he's at Cassadaga!"

The kid's eyes weren't right. He was on something, it occurred to Greg, something that made him different than he had been the other day, when he'd run from Greg like Greg was the weird one. Now he bobbed his knee up and down and he smelled like the stagnant creek that ran out behind Greg's house. The color of his gums, which he flashed often, was too pink, too vibrant. Cassadaga was where the kooks gathered. Greg had been the accountant for a woman who owned two palm-reader storefronts in Orlando, and she called Cassadaga the last stop on the Looneyville Express. All his life, if he worked hard enough, he'd been able to make something happen. School, work, women. Sometimes he didn't even have to work all that hard; he'd just have to bend a finger at someone and whatever he wanted was his. He had done the work, the past few days. He'd looked for GJ the best way he knew how. There was even a missing persons report now, if Marie had done what she said she would. Yet here he was, again, asking himself what in the ever-loving fuck he was doing.

"I'm sorry," Greg said. "I can't drive you."

"Oh, really?" the kid said mildly, like Greg had just told him his favorite food was Italian.

"Yeah, I'm really sorry." He began slowing down, pulling over to the shoulder. If he rushed he could make it home by midnight, or he could spend the night and make it home mid-morning. He'd give this kid some money, maybe even his phone number, in case the kid got in a bind.

"Why are you slowing down?" the kid asked. He was hunched down, holding his own legs like he was bracing for impact.

"I'm going to let you out," Greg said. The kid seemed to need things spelled out for him. GJ was never like that; he was quick. Maybe that's why he was such a good liar. "This is all just a waste of time. I've just been wasting time, this whole time. Time, time, time," he said, laughing, hoping the kid would think he was a batty old man he'd be glad to be rid of. But then he felt something run down his arm, like a pen that wrote fire, and when he looked he saw that instead of flames there was blood. The kid had a knife, something small and sharp, was hacking and slicing at his arm and shoulder like a child playing swords. For a sickening moment Greg let the wheel go, his foot coming off the gas, his whole body attempting to float up up up in the thick sludge of those few seconds, like he was at the bottom of the ocean trying to surface for air. But then the kid cut him from ear to cheek, the fire sweeping across his face now, and Greg brought his foot down hard on the brake. The RV shrieked; the kid lurched sideways into the dashboard. The knife flew out of his hand, hitting the windshield and falling into Greg's lap, smeared with his own blood. The kid was holding his ear and Greg reached across and pushed the door open, then leaned back and kicked him with both feet, over and over, the kid howling and trying to stop Greg's feet with his backpack, until finally the kid fell out. Greg rammed the gas and swerved onto the highway, the passenger door swinging wildly and finally slamming closed from the momentum.

The RV wasn't going fast enough; he had the pedal all the way to the floor but still the world crept by. His face singed and throbbing but his neck tickled by his blood. He looked in the rearview; he looked again and again but he saw nothing. He was sobbing, he realized. Heaving. He saw a sign for a BP and pulled off, but he had to coax his foot to ease up on the pedal. He screeched into one of the two parking spots they had by the convenience store. He watched out the window, scared the kid had followed him, knew where he was. Finally, he felt calm enough to do something about the blood. He mopped his face and arm as best he could with GJ's sweatpants, then gingerly pulled on the long-sleeved button-down that had been wadded under the dinette. He wanted to hide his flayed arm; he didn't feel he had the right to bleed in front of the attendant or the customers. The cuts hurt and he was still breathing heavily, but if he could just get to a sink, some soap and some Band-Aids . . . They had to have some kind of bandage for sale among the bags of hard candy and the sunflower seeds and decks of cards that every gas station seemed to sell. He pushed his door open and half fell out of the RV. His legs felt gummy with adrenaline and he could feel his cheek getting wet with blood again. He put his phone up to that ear to hide the cut. There was an older man pumping gas into his car; a boxy blue minivan pulled to the adjacent pump and seemed to spill children out of its side maw like it was spitting teeth.

"Mm-hmm," Greg said into his phone. "Sure." A digital thermometer over the door said it was 95 degrees out; the children's hair clung to their faces with sweat, but for once Greg felt mercifully cool. He longed to wipe his face but he was afraid that any motion would make him shoot all his blood out like a sprinkler. Once inside, he found the sign for the bathroom at the other end of the store and started making his way there. "Well, we'll have to see," he said into his phone. His neck felt wet now; he hoped the collar of his shirt was hiding the gore. His sleeve felt stuck to his arm. He shivered; the air-conditioning in the place was on full blast, humming over him in a breathy, aggressive chant.

"You must buy something," the attendant said, not even looking up at Greg from the magazine she was reading. *Penthouse*, was it a *Penthouse*?

"I'm good for twenty dollars' gas and a couple lotto tickets once I get out," he said. He'd left his wallet in the RV again but he'd figure that out after he got cleaned up. He wanted to kiss the attendant for not giving a shit about him, for not looking up to take him in. For once he was glad not to be acknowledged.

The bathroom was only a bit more spacious than the shower in the RV, with a single bulb blaring out over the mirror. He looked half-bearded with blood, but the cut was already congealing in places, attempting to close itself. Greg blotted at it with a blossom of wet toilet paper that quickly became pink. He folded a few squares into a bandage and stuck that directly to the cut, stanching what remained of the blood so he could concentrate on his arm. He peeled the shirt slowly down. His arm didn't so much hurt as it glittered with pain. There were nicks and slashes from his shoulder to his wrist, and a few longer or deeper gashes along his biceps. One looked like a lipless mouth, helpless against its pulse of blood. It was goddamned freezing cold, Greg's whole body in a spasm of shivering. His cell phone was on the sink ledge and it fell in a clatter. He could hear a voice saying *Hello? Hello? You there?* It sounded like Deb's voice, and Greg reached to pick up the phone but fell to his knees instead, smashing his nose on the sink and then crumpling down to take a nap, which seemed like the only thing to do in this cold evil dungeon painted with his own blood.

You were in shock," the doctor was saying. "You should thank your lucky stars those kids found you when they did."

Greg was propped up with pillows that felt filled with air, collapsing and collapsing and doing nothing to help relieve the flat pain in his ass. He'd been lying in this position awhile, he gathered. His right arm was cocooned in white bandages; his jaw ached under its own bandage.

"Kids?"

"Right," the doctor said. He was in green scrubs, which made Greg think he wasn't a real doctor, not yet; real doctors had white coats. "Are you ready to tell us what happened?"

Greg looked around. It was only him and the doctor in the room. There was no *us* that he could see. He remembered the boy's warm hand on his arm, the faded blue in his eyes, the way he'd finally fallen out of the car with a thud Greg remembered hearing even over the traffic.

"You should see the other guy," Greg said, and tried to smile.

The doctor didn't smile back. He looked tired, with dry lips and thick dark lines under his eyes. His shirt was wrinkled, like he'd slept in it. "Well, aside from being stabbed," the doctor said, the word *stabbed* ringing in Greg's ears like a gunshot, "it looks like you recently had a heart attack. Did you know that?"

Greg tried to remember. All he could think of was how he'd left his body for a second, just one tiny second, while he was on the floor with Marie. How he left it again when the kid cut him. How everything felt off, like he was watching life through a lens. How he never fully caught his breath.

"It was a small one, but you'll have another one very soon if you aren't careful." Greg hung his head, rubbed the back of his neck. He really was exhausted; his ravaged blubber graveyard of a body wasn't doing him any favors. The doctor took a deep breath. "Also, your liver is slightly engorged and your blood pressure is too high. Your blood alcohol was approaching the legal limit and the EMTs said your pockets were filled with wrappers. You're not a young man," he said, coming closer to Greg's bedside. "If the stabbing didn't kill you, your lifestyle is well on its way."

Greg had tipped a small bottle of whiskey into his sweet tea that morning; that was true. It wasn't like he was taking shots. It took longer to think through the wrappers, remember exactly what they could have been. They were probably from the KFC and Pizza Hut. Then he remembered the plastic bag of Hostess cupcakes he'd been keeping in his duffel and replenishing when he could. And the candy bars he lined the glove compartment with. He held them one by one in front of the air-conditioning vents to bring their melty bodies back up to solids, peeled the wrappers off with the usual difficulty, like how it must feel to skin a rabbit. And the LifeSavers he kept on hand, to mask the whiskey. And the tiny snack-size bags of Fritos when he needed some salt, which was a lot lately, what with all the sweating. There was also the refrigerated storage bench in the dinette, which he'd stuffed with hot dogs and bologna and bricks of sliced cheese. Hawaiian rolls and cheesecakes. Most of it was gone now, eaten on the drive; Greg ferreting out the next victim at each stop for gas, or when Marie scuttled away from him the morning he drove to his father's, or after he left his father's, when he felt so hungry that he ate until he threw up, a soup of tacos and hot dogs and yeasty rolls pouring out of him into the empty King's bag. Or in the early hours of the parking lot outside the strip club, when the sky was the color of dust on a bureau, when he hadn't been hungry at all but felt so trapped between the nothing he'd driven away from and the nothing before him that he'd eaten an entire cheesecake with his fingers, which was truly the best way to eat anything, and then washed it down with a four-ounce bottle of rum, not even enough to get one of Deb's porcelain dolls tipsy. He'd gone to the strip club to distract himself. To hide from the bench. Eat only when you're hungry, the diets all said. Okay. Okay, okay. Greg ate when he was hungry.

The last time he'd seen GJ, that rainy Christmas Eve, he was down sixty pounds. He'd been on the no-carb plan, had even started walking the trails that wound behind his house. He was excited for GJ to see him, the new him. But none of it had mattered. And now he had gained that sixty back, plus another forty—a hundred pounds in a matter of months. At any moment it felt like the ground underneath him would bow and snap, no longer able to support such an enormous blob, and he'd tumble, flailing, into the fireball center of the earth. He didn't need this doctor with his toned arms and haggard face to tell him he was killing himself. *Greg is becoming chubby.* His father didn't say a thing in response. Not a thing.

"I used to steal food," Greg said. "My mother never ate. I think she thought it made people look weak. I'd go to my friend's house and while he was in the bathroom or watching television I'd shove food down my pants or under my shirt. Then I'd hide it under my bed so I could eat it at night when my mom was asleep. I even kept a bag of dry rice under there, just in case. I got fat and then my mom stopped even pretending to make dinner. So I stole food from the grocery store. We had one a couple blocks away and I'd go in and buy coffee or flowers, make it seem like an errand for my mother, but really I'd be walking out with my pockets stuffed with candy or those little wheels of cheese. Sometimes I'd take it into the bathroom they had and eat it all there, so I wouldn't have to walk out with it." He was crying now, a real mess, he could almost see himself in the doctor's eyes. Stubbled chins. Fleshy pectorals. Barrel of belly under the gown. Tears that were more grease than salt. His pale, pale feet, sticking out of the blanket like plucked chickens.

The doctor put his hand on Greg's shoulder. "Eating is an essential part of the human experience." He patted Greg lightly. "But everything in moderation. Including beating yourself up."

Greg nodded. His tears were stinging the cut on his cheek and he wanted them to stop, but they flowed endlessly on.

"What if I told you my own mother said I'd burn in hell with all the rest of the faggots?" the doctor asked. His eyes looked too dry and the word *faggots* rang out like a second gunshot.

"I'd tell you your mother needed help," Greg said. "And not to listen to her."

The doctor nodded. "There you go." He leaned over to check Greg's bandages, pulling the one on his cheek out so he could look at the cut. "I'm going to have a nurse come in and re-dress this. In the meantime, is there anyone you'd like me to call?" the doctor asked. "Your wife? Your family?"

"My son," Greg said. He could barely get the words out; the tears were choking him, bursting from his face.

"Write his number down," the doctor said, and Greg did, with his left hand, the numbers looking like someone had bent each into shape from a paper clip, even though he knew there wasn't much of a point. GJ's phone had been off for weeks. The doctor walked quickly out and soon the nurse came in, tending to Greg's face with a gentle purpose that made him cry all over again.

"When you've suffered an attack, it's normal to cry a lot," she said. Had it been an attack, what he'd experienced with the kid? It had felt like a misunderstanding, something that went just a bit too far. Then his cheek and biceps sang out together, a shriek from a bullhorn, and he remembered he was not the one with the knife. "Then you'll feel rage," the nurse was saying. "Then, probably, you'll be depressed for a little while." Her hands smelled like rosemary and garlic, and Greg wanted to tell her she was describing his whole life. She taped a wedge of cotton just under his eye. "This will catch your tears, like a little hammock."

He thanked her. "Just doing my job," she said, but it felt beyond that; it felt like everyone but him knew he was a child. She left and he was alone. He realized he wasn't even sure what hospital he was at—one in Orlando, or one farther north? He looked around for a clue, a pad of paper or a pamphlet, but there was nothing. He thought of Deb, how he'd have to call her and explain the cuts and gashes, how he hadn't spoken to her in what felt like a lifetime. She was peace; she was silence and order. But he hadn't missed her all that much. Maybe that was a good sign; it meant they were content together and didn't need constant contact to remain that way. Or maybe it meant another thing, something he felt too old to consider. He felt worn almost to death, as craggy and empty as a cave.

The doctor came back in, wearing a different set of scrubs now, less wrinkled and with a logo over the heart. HealthCentral, it said. Ocoee, FL. So he was back in central Florida.

"He didn't pick up, so I left a message," the doctor said. "I told him how to reach me and what room you're in. I can try again on my next break, if you want."

"You got his voice mail?" Greg asked. He hadn't gotten GJ's voice mail since the first week he'd gone missing. After that it had told him the number wasn't available and hung up on him.

"Right," the doctor said.

"Where's my cell phone?" Greg asked. He looked around but didn't see his clothes anywhere, his wallet, nothing of his.

"Ah," the doctor said. "I believe it's at the desk with some of your other things, but the nurses told me it got a bit wet."

It had clattered into the sink at the BP, Greg remembered.

"It might not be in the best shape," the doctor went on. "But I can bring you a phone to use."

"Can I just have my things?" Greg asked. "And where is my RV?"

"Hmm. I'd imagine it's either still at the gas station or it's been towed."

"Shit."

"I'll ask around. The cops usually show up after a few hours to take statements, so you could ask them about it at that point, too." The doctor looked at his watch, impatient to move on, and Greg waved him off. "I'll be back later," he said, the door swinging shut behind him.

A voice mail. So GJ's phone was back on? A male nurse brought him a phone to use, plugging it into the wall by his bed and standing too close as Greg dialed.

"Hello?" A woman's annoyed voice.

"Um." Greg's voice was thick and pebbled. He cleared his throat. "May I please speak to GJ?"

"Ain't no GJ here," the voice said. She sucked her teeth. Greg could hear what sounded like a television in the background, a game show, maybe, a large crowd screaming and clapping.

"What about Greg? Or Gregory?" It felt strange, saying his own name into the phone. Asking if Greg was there. The nurse pulled his blanket tight, tucking it underneath him, like he was a sarcophagus.

"Ain't here," the voice said.

"Not there right now? Or not there at all?" Greg felt that underwater feeling again, like he was trying to kick to the surface but had misjudged the timing and wouldn't make it. He kicked free from the blankets, sat on the edge of the bed.

"Mr. Reinart," the nurse said, warning edging his voice. He pushed lightly on Greg's shoulders, careful not to push on his wounds. Greg pushed back; sometimes his considerable heft worked in his favor.

"Ain't. Here," the voice said again. Greg could hear another television now, this one with the rigid timbre of a female news anchor's voice. A bar, the woman was at a bar, somewhere with competing televisions, somewhere open in the daytime.

"Who is this?" Greg asked. He held the nurse at bay with his foot so he could pull the IV out of his arm. The electrodes were easier, but their wires got tangled as he pulled them from under his shirt, and he dropped the receiver in the chaos. When he picked it back up, the dial tone rang out. It had felt like he was trapped in the Bermuda Triangle of central Florida, pulled in the wrong directions again and again by some unseen force. But now there was finally an answer on the other end of the line.

"Sir," the nurse was shouting. Greg pushed past him, running around the foot of the bed and toward the door. He was in a hospital gown, open at the back, but they'd blessedly left his undershorts on. He could think of only one place there was left to look, a place he knew GJ could go and find help. He was running now, down the hall, toward the nurse's station. He felt like laughing, the canned air tasting almost sweet as it filled his mouth and lungs. The male nurse was not chasing him but he ran harder, the hall seeming to stretch and the nurse's station moving swiftly, cleverly away from him. "Aha!" he shouted, and ran harder. Thirty steps, then forty, then fifty. With every step, his cuts throbbed and whined. Seventy, a hundred. He estimated only about thirty left, and he was nearly correct. Twenty-eight and he was square in front of two nurses behind the counter, each wearing pale peach scrubs and looking at him with bored, slack faces.

"I'm leaving," he panted. "I need my stuff. Greg Reinart." He pointed at himself.

"Well, we can't make you stay," one of the nurses said. "But it's probably not in your best interests to leave." She turned to open a locked drawer, pulled a clear bag out containing his shoes, his cell phone, and his wallet.

"I'll come back," Greg said. "Promise."

The other nurse had been watching him, and she shrugged, looking back down at her computer monitor.

"You have to be admitted," the first nurse said. "You can't just come back and check yourself in."

"Right," Greg said.

"Meaning you have to have suffered an *event*." She tossed the bag onto the counter.

"My clothes?" Greg asked.

Both nurses looked at him, like he'd just told a joke. "They cut them off you," said the second nurse. She covered Greg's hand with her own. "They're gone," she said firmly, as if reminding a kook that his loved one had died decades ago.

"Right," Greg said again.

The first nurse went back to the drawer. "Here," she said. She pulled plastic-wrapped scrubs out. "These should fit. You can't walk around with your . . . like that."

Greg pulled the scrubs on in the hallway, which meant he was nearly naked in front of these young, pretty women, the pale mammoth of his torso exposed, pocked with moles and hairs. But only for a moment; he was quick. He felt thankful that the neck hole was large enough to prevent the fabric from scraping his wounded face. The top was short-sleeved, another blessing. He folded the gown neatly and handed it to the second nurse, who pushed her wheeled chair over to a hamper and dropped it in.

The male nurse made it to the station just then. He put his hands up. "It's your funeral," he said. The first nurse snickered.

"Gallows humor," the second nurse said, as if they were all looking at a rare bird and she'd just thought of the name.

"Have a good day," Greg said. He no longer felt like running, the appearance of the male nurse reminding him that the doctor had said he'd had a heart attack. His heart suddenly felt raw in his chest, like it had been tenderized with a mallet, like it could shrivel or burble wetly from his throat at any moment. He managed a brisk walk and felt relieved when he turned the corner and could no longer feel their eyes on his back.

The waiting area in the downstairs lobby was filled with people. Children playing in a stingy Kids Korner, where there were tattered *Highlights* and a nicked bead maze; adults asleep with their mouths open; an elderly man hunched over, making no attempt to hide a deep gash in his forehead. Greg wondered if his vacancy meant one of these people might get a shot at seeing a doctor now, and he walked even faster. The pneumatic doors hissed at his approach and again as they closed behind him. He squinted; everywhere he turned it seemed the sun was glaring down at him as blinding as a camera flash. He shielded his eyes and checked his phone. Its screen showed hash marks and dashes; it could no longer dial or retrieve voice mails. It was officially dead. Greg inserted it tenderly into the slot of a garbage can at the curb, listened as it whumped down into what sounded like a soft landing, for which he was grateful. Deb would be thrilled to know he'd need a new phone; she'd want him to buy one of those phones that had no keypads, the ones with the icons that were just a smidge too small for his thick fingers. Fine, fine, he thought to himself. No biggie. I'll get used to it and it'll make Deb happy. What day was today? It was hard to remember; it was hard to dredge up the same feelings he'd had when he started this trip. But he had a destination in mind, one that felt so obvious now, and there was a taxi idling just beyond the garbage can.

Greg leaned into the open passenger-side window. "Can you take me?" he asked.

"You Jessica?" the driver asked. He held a word search in his lap, a gnawed golf pencil poised just above it.

"Sure," Greg said.

"Works for me," the driver said. "I've been waiting over seven minutes."

Greg liked a man who remembered the details, who said *seven minutes* instead of rounding down to five or up to ten. "Great," he said, and got into the backseat. It smelled like oranges in there, fresh and clean, and Greg could have kissed the driver.

Only ten minutes later they pulled into the vast parking lot of the shopping plaza where Mick's was located. It was feeling more and more like fate that Greg hadn't been able to escape the orbit of central Florida, and that the hospital was in Ocoee, such a short drive from Mick's.

"This it?" the driver asked. Greg had told him how to get there, turn by turn, as if Mick's was his childhood home and the route there was part of who he was, indelibly etched into his brain the way the steps for tying a shoe were. As they pulled in there had been the Publix, the Cato, the Cato PLUS, the Gymboree, the Blockbuster—empty inside, Greg could see—and then, where Mick's had been, there was something else. Its tall brick façade held melon-colored letters that felt dwarfed in comparison, and they read CROC'S WATERING SPOT. Beyond the darkly tinted windows he could just make out slanted televisions peering down from the ceiling like flickering gargoyles. Greg looked around, out into the parking lot, beyond to the roads bordering the plaza on each side. This was definitely where it had been, but it was not here now.

"You remember a place called Mick's?" he asked the driver.

The driver met Greg's eye in the rearview. "This isn't my part of town," he said.

Greg thought of asking to be driven back to the hospital, or over to Marie's, or back to the BP to see if the RV was there, but all of those options felt hazy, like they were hallways in a dream.

He held his debit card out to the driver and the driver sighed as if he'd handed over a plate of dung.

"I only have a dollar in cash," Greg said to the back of the driver's wagging head, but it didn't seem to help.

The crocodile theme carried on inside, which Greg saw as soon as his eyes adjusted to the darkness. It seemed the main source of light came from the televisions and the window, which provided only so much, what with the thick brown tint. There was synthetic swamp grass along the bar and a huge painting of a crocodile above the bottles. Three mounted crocodile heads, one of which Greg thought might be an alligator instead, were mounted above the hostess's station inside the door. When it had been Mick's there was no hostess station, there was only one television that hung behind the bar, and the only theme it could have been mistaken for was *yard sale*.

There was news on one of the televisions; the credits to *The Price Is Right* were rolling on another. He looked around for the woman who'd answered GJ's phone. There was a blonde at the bar in a cheap suit with boxy shoulders, there was the hostess smiling at him like he was the one to offer her a seat, and there was a plump woman hunched over, her back to him, three booths back. None of them were holding a cell phone.

"Is there a man here by the name of GJ?" Greg asked the hostess. She had short curly hair and a small gold earring clutching her eyebrow.

"Do you mean DJ?" the hostess asked. She had a menu clutched to her breast like it was a schoolbook. "DJ doesn't work on Tuesdays."

So it was Tuesday. Yesterday, Monday, he'd fought off the kid. A whole night had passed without him knowing it. *Today is Tuesday, that much I know.*

"Not DJ. G. GJ," Greg said. "He's my son."

"Hmm, well, let's see," she said, as if she could help him pick something off the menu, as if the menu might offer something just as good as his son. "I can ask the manager." Before Greg could answer she walked off, disappearing behind double doors that hadn't existed in the days of Mick's. Greg walked over to the blonde, who was in the process of lighting a thin cigarette. Greg cupped his hand over the flame, which was what GJ would have called *creepy*, he knew it as soon as he did it, the blonde's eyes sweeping his mummified arm. He had only been trying to ingratiate himself.

"May I see your cell phone?" he asked.

She blew a stream of smoke from her pursed lips. Greg looked down at the gold locket she wore, the letter M in its tarnished center. "I'm not up for talking," she said. Her face was pretty enough, with a strong chin and a dainty nose and big liquidy brown eyes, but there was a mole the size of a boll weevil melting down her upper lip. Even so, Greg guessed she got hit on a lot in bars.

"Me either," he said. He stepped back a bit and raised his hands to show her he didn't want a thing, only her cell phone. "I just want to see your cell phone. I don't even have to touch it," he added. Out of the corner of his eye he could see the hostess and the manager walking around the bar toward him.

"Hey," the woman said. "I said no."

"But you didn't say no," Greg said. He felt like she was purposefully misunderstanding him, like she wasn't listening, couldn't see how badly he needed her help. "You did not say the word *no*."

"You can't smoke in here," the hostess said. She and the manager, a pear-shaped butch by the looks of it, were now standing in between Greg and the blonde, who dropped the butt into her beer bottle.

"I was only asking if I could see her cell phone," Greg said. His tattered heart, barely hanging on. He felt like someone was cutting the strings, one by one, and it was slumping farther into his gut, where his stomach would make quick work of it. It moaned in anticipation but the women didn't seem to hear. He put his hand over his sternum, to protect it from the harpies before him.

"We got a phone in the office that you can use," the manager said. She put a hand on his elbow, tried to lead him away. The blonde gathered her purse and cigarettes and hopped off her bar stool and walked away, toward the door.

"I don't want to see the phone in the office!" Greg bellowed. "I want to see her phone!" He pointed at the retreating woman, who was swallowed by the daylight. "And hers!" He pointed at Plumpy hunched over her plate. "And yours!" He pointed at the hostess, who held the menu out like a shield now.

"Sir, that's not going to happen," the manager said. She pulled his elbow harder now and *snip*, his heart dropped like a stone, right into a pool of acid. He heaved for air, like he was retching in reverse, but none came through. He felt his cheeks sinking inward with the effort. He clutched at the manager; he clawed at the hostess, slapping the menu from her hands. Darkness was crowding in all around him, the way it swallows all but a star. He went to his knees, opening the scab he'd gotten in Marie's parking lot. The bar stools honked and tumbled. Everything was the same; he'd never escape this fruitless trip. His son being the fruit. Not what I meant! He tried to scream it at the women but they watched him melt into the sticky, gritty floor as if he were a vaporizing cockroach. His heart must be a puddle by now. *Night night*, that's how GJ said it as a boy. *Night night, Mama. Night night, Dada.*

Greg always impatient for the boy to go to sleep, leave him alone. Now he was alone. Before Greg went night night at the feet of the two women, he thought with no small amount of wonder that maybe this was what he'd hungered for, year after year. To consume his own heart and be done with it.

It was late spring but there was a smell of ashes and a clap of bitterness to the air. Greg had opened his window to feel the sun on his face but ended up closing it quickly. Not that he didn't welcome the brace; it was interesting, nice even, to expect warmth but be greeted with ice. He welcomed the gentle disorientation; he welcomed the cold, so opposite of the close heat of Florida. It reminded him that time would continue plodding along, day to day, season to season. Soon it would be summer, then autumn, then winter . . . time would pass. It was a certainty, a comfort.

Deb was still in the house. He could hear the groaning floor-boards downstairs as she walked from the kitchen to the porch, probably filling her bird feeders, as she did every Wednesday. She was afraid to leave him alone for too long, he knew. She'd flown down to collect him—her word, *collect*, as if he were a tax. She'd used their miles, miles they'd talked about using to visit wine country or Hawaii someday. Instead she'd had to gouge them to fly down and be met at the airport by Marie, and then be driven to the hospital by Marie, and then hear from the doctor that he'd attacked someone in a bar and then had a panic attack. She'd had to take a taxi to the tow lot where the RV was, had to pay for it to be professionally cleaned of the rotting food and moldy cups and puddles of blood and the sewage that had burbled up through the shower drain and dried. She described all of this to him later, when they'd been home a few days, speaking gently to him, every sentence with a tentative question mark at the end of it. *And there was food, so much food? And there were empty bottles?* As if she was asking him to remember, begging him to confirm it all for her. He had just showered; his hair was too long and was wetting his shirt collar. His feet were bare. The couch had given in underneath him as it always had. Deb had made them mugs of tea. The trees outside hushed each other. This was home; Deb was home. Still, he couldn't hold back the urge to want to shout, to yell, *So?* To ask her why she believed everything had to make sense. Instead he sat silently, nodding, his hands upturned in his lap. They hadn't worked well since Florida. He could no longer make a satisfying fist. He still didn't know where GJ was and he couldn't shake the feeling that it was Deb's fault. She'd put a stop to it all, brought him home. Exactly where he didn't want to be, it turned out.

He opened the window again. Where did he want to be? His face began to sting from the cold. Nowhere.

He and Deb had driven the RV back over the course of two days, spending the night in a Sherwood Inn that smelled like a hot Band-Aid. Mostly he'd slept, or pretended to sleep. He saw a sign for a place called Eat 'n' See and couldn't recall if that was the same place he'd stopped his first night on the road, a hundred lifetimes ago. Deb was good at letting him be, at not asking questions, or maybe he was giving her too much credit. Maybe she just didn't want to know.

"Well, this will all make sense with time," Deb had said that day on the couch. "There's a purpose for everything." And over the coming days, she'd hung a leather strap laden with bells on the door to the pantry and trashed all the alcohol in the house, even the gooed-up bottle of NyQuil that had been in the downstairs bathroom for years. The pastor at her church even came to dinner one Friday night, glopped Deb's taco casserole onto his plate while telling Greg about the men's group and the AA meetings the church offered. "Nothing to be ashamed of," the pastor said. There was a bean stuck midway up the man's fork, and Greg waited for the man to catch it with each bite, but there it remained. Greg laughed until tears rolled down his cheeks. Deb stood to offer the store-bought flan but the pastor said he didn't have a sweet tooth. Deb walked him out and Greg watched as they hugged for just a smidge too long, the pastor's hand at the back of Deb's head, their bodies touching from shoulders to knees. He surprised himself by feeling flooded with relief, for her and for himself.

He went downstairs. Deb was still on the porch, hanging her feeders. He opened the pantry, holding the leather strap in his hand to dull the chimes. Multigrain crackers, a jar of purple olives, a box of Grape-Nuts. He took a handful of the crackers; a difficult seed immediately got caught in his molar. It should have been the end, is what it came down to. In his heart, he was sorry he hadn't died on the floor of that bar. He'd thought he was dying and he had not, and it was not a polite kind of disorientation. It was not making sense with time.

He dialed GJ's number and got a recording explaining that

the number was no longer in service. He had not heard from Marie and had not tried to call.

Deb came in from the porch, bringing a sail of icy wind with her. "Aren't those interesting?" she asked, looking at the crackers. "I found them in the healthy aisle."

"They're great," he said. The seed felt like a rock he'd never loosen. This was the kind of conversation they had now, Deb afraid to say anything real and Greg playing the part of a doddering, harmless old man.

"What would you like for dinner?" Deb asked. "Soup and sandwiches? Some kind of noodles? We could have eggs and potatoes . . ."

"Why don't we go out?" It was his way of challenging her. Going out meant the proximity of junk food. The possibility of booze.

"Oh," she said, drifting off.

"Soup sounds good," he said. She smiled, relieved. "Can I ask you," he went on, "about Pastor Lawrence?" His heart began to thunder; he hadn't planned on saying that.

"About the meetings?" Deb asked.

"No . . ." He stopped himself. Beyond the windows, the trees were tossing about, the green leaves so new, so bright that they hurt his eyes. He would never tell Deb about that night with Marie. "Yes, about the meetings."

She went over to a drawer and pulled out a yellow pad of paper. "I wrote down the times. There is one tonight at five-thirty—that's the AA one—and a men's group meeting in the morning on Saturday."

He had received a letter about three days after returning home. A letter, of all things. Where had GJ gotten a stamp? Where had he gotten an envelope? The postmark was smudged; it was difficult to tell what the zip code was. Greg had read it standing over the sink in his kitchen, listening to the uneven *drip dripdrip drip* that had lately begun to infuriate him. The letter was typed. Where had GJ gotten access to a computer? A printer?

Dad, I reject your narrative.

The gist of the letter was forgiveness. GJ forgave him; GJ rejected Greg's version of the story. What story?

We're both addicts.

Greg had held the letter under the dripping faucet, watching it grow soggy, willing the words to fade. When it finally fell away from his hand and landed in the sink, he turned the water on, and then he pushed the letter down the garbage disposal with the handle of a wooden spoon. He did not mention the letter to Deb, or Marie, and after a few days he'd decided it had never happened, was just a fantasy he had manufactured in his desperate urge to connect with his son.

"Maybe I'll go tonight," he said. "Live a little."

"I love it," Deb said. It was clear it'd shaken her, his bringing up Pastor Lawrence. She smiled too big, pushed her voice too hard. One of the dining chairs was askew; had she and the pastor done it under the table?

In the car on the way down the mountain, the afternoon light felt sharp, too bright, every leaf and pebble forcing itself into Greg's view. He took the curves slowly, squinting, every now and again waving his hand in front of his face as if he could shoo away the brightness. Would he really go to the meeting? No, probably not. "Maybe we can have barbecue tonight," Deb had said. "You could stop at Piggy's on the way back." He probably wouldn't do that, either. Where was he going? *Nowhere.* When he was a boy, his dog had disappeared one day and never come back. *He went off to find a place to die*, his father had told him, as if it was something Greg should have known. *That's what old dogs do.* It had hurt him back then, imagining the dog dying alone. Now that kind of solitude felt like just the thing. Two more turns and he'd reach the bottom of the mountain, could drive faster, escape the light whipping into his eyes around every turn.

If he was honest with himself, there was a part of him that felt proud of GJ for the letter. Glad. Like he'd been a glue trap holding GJ in place, as his son, as a problem, as something predefined and predictable and forever doomed. GJ had freed himself. Greg had driven off and boomeranged right back to where he started. GJ was the unknown now, Greg the known. But really, weren't they all? Marie, Deb, GJ. Impossible to know them with any finality. Impossible to hold them. He felt a sharpness in his eye— the salt of a tear? Or maybe it was just that it hurt to look now. It hurt to see. *Good for him*, he was thinking. *Good for him*.

ACKNOWLEDGMENTS

This book was made possible by the generosity of:

My mother-in-law, Sue Brockett, who has supported my writing career in every sense of the word from the day I mentioned I might like to go study writing, like, for real.

NogginLabs, Inc., which is so much more than a day job and is run by the amazing humans Traci and Brian Knudson, who push their employees to creative excellence both in and outside the office. All four of my books were written while I was employed there, and I don't think that's a coincidence.

My brilliant and crazy editor, Emily Bell, who has championed my work and spoiled me rotten.

My agent, Jim Rutman, whose thoughtful reading and patient phone calls buoyed and challenged me.

Jac Jemc and Kyle Beachy, who read early drafts of this book and offered invaluable insight and excitement.

My son Parker, who got shipped off to the sitter many, many days so I could write. I live to make you and your baby brother proud of me.

My husband, Ben, who watches me tear my hair out and eat bags of candy bars and slouch around in despair, and knows that this is my process and makes room for it and loves me anyway.

Thank you, thank you to all of the above. I am the luckiest.

A Note About the Author

Lindsay Hunter cofounded and cohosted the groundbreaking Quickies! reading series, a monthly event that focused on flash fiction. Her first book, *Daddy's,* a collection of flash fiction, was published in 2010 by Featherproof Books, a boutique press in Chicago. Her second collection, *Don't Kiss Me,* was published by FSG Originals in 2013 and was named one of Amazon's 10 Best Short Story Collections of the Year. Her first novel, *Ugly Girls,* was published by Farrar, Straus and Giroux in 2014. *The Huffington Post* called it "a story that hits a note that's been missing from the chorus of existing feminist literature." She lives in Chicago with her beloved husband, sons, and dogs.